"What are you doing?" Annie asked drowsily

"Taking off my shirt." Sam settled back down beside her again, pulling her close. She felt him fumbling with the front of her dress, slipping buttons through holes.

"You promised you wouldn't do that anymore," she managed to say.

"I lied." He kissed her once more, a tender, almost apologetic caress, filled with frightening finality. "I'm sorry, Annie. It's out of my hands now."

"What do you mean?" And then she heard it. Heard the angry voices and the stomp of feet. "Oh, no!" The door to the boathouse crashed inward.

"Annie! Annie, are you all right?"

"I'm fine, Bertie. But could you—?"

"She's here!" the deputy shouted to those behind him. "And so's Sam. He's finally done it, boys. He's compromised Annie. Get the preacher. There's gonna be a wedding!"

WHITE
WEDDINGS

True love is worth waiting for...

Dear Reader,

Welcome to a wonderful, brand-new miniseries,
WHITE WEDDINGS. Everyone loves a wedding, with all
the excitement of the big day: bedecked bridesmaids,
festive flowers, champagne and all the emotions of the
happy couple exchanging vows....

Some of your favorite authors will be bringing you all this
and more in a special selection of Harlequin Romance®
novels. You'll meet blushing brides and gorgeous grooms,
all with one thing in common: for better or worse, they are
determined the bride should wear white on her wedding
day...which means keeping passions in check!

Happy Reading!

The Editors

Look out for our next WHITE WEDDING
A Wedding Worth Waiting For
by Jessica Steele (#3569)

Shotgun Bridegroom
Day Leclaire

TORONTO • NEW YORK • LONDON
AMSTERDAM • PARIS • SYDNEY • HAMBURG
STOCKHOLM • ATHENS • TOKYO • MILAN • MADRID
PRAGUE • WARSAW • BUDAPEST • AUCKLAND

ISBN 0-373-03564-0

SHOTGUN BRIDEGROOM

First North American Publication 1999.

Copyright © 1999 by Day Totton Smith.

PROLOGUE

EVEN after a seven-year absence, Sam Beaumont could still make the residents of Delacorte Island nervous. Year after year, he hung offshore like a distant hurricane, growing ever larger and stronger, while edging relentlessly closer. It wasn't entirely unexpected that one day he'd come roaring off the local ferry on the back of his black Harley and into the town of Beaumont—a town that had been named after his pirating ancestors by the colonial mayor. Of course, the fact that the poor mayor had a gun to his head may have had something to do with his impromptu decision.

Nor was it unexpected that on a bright and sunny July morning, Sam Beaumont would demand to see the three men responsible for running him off the island—especially since it, too, had been at gunpoint. After all, the small North Carolina island was well accustomed to the destructive force of hurricanes. Whenever they struck, the townsfolk battened down and prepared to ride out the storm. And this promised to be quite a storm.

"He's come to ruin us, now that he's rich," Mayor Jeffrey Pike announced gloomily. "We never should have run him out of town, Rolly."

Sheriff Rawling glowered. "He could have turned right around and ridden back in. I wasn't planning on stoppin' the boy. Were you?"

"Stop a Beaumont? Not likely," the third member of their group, Ben Drake, piped up. "I have a business to consider. Wouldn't do to get a reputation for running people off, now would it? Not when I want them buying their groceries and fishing tackle from me.''

Rolly chuckled. ''No fear there, Ben. Ever'body in these parts knows you're a sucker for a hard-luck story. Why you've offered your hand in friendship to so many people, it's a wonder it hasn't been shook clean off.''

''Except for Beaumont,'' Ben retorted.

''Well, now. That's a different story altogether. Young Beaumont wasn't interested in no hand of friendship.''

''Yes sirree, that hand was a mite busy with other things,'' Mayor Pike offered with a hearty chuckle. ''Like seeing how many women he could—''

''Exactly,'' Ben interrupted. ''And what with our Annie next on his list, we had to do something, didn't we?''

Rolly nodded. ''Absolutely. We had no choice in the matter. She asked for help and we give it to her. Runnin' that boy out of town was the least we could do. No harm came of it. Why, Sam made a name for himself, right? If anything, we did him a favor.''

''Sure did, Rolly. We surely did.'' Mayor Pike glanced uneasily from one to the other. ''You suppose he's come to get even for that favor we did him?''

Ben Drake gave his friends a morose look. ''Why else would he have asked to see the three of us? Can't be any other reason.''

Further discussion ended the minute Sam Beaumont strode into Mayor Pike's office. Seven years had wrought changes in the man—though none that reassured the three. He was still tall, graceful and disgustingly handsome. But in the years since they'd last seen him, he'd added several impressive inches to his chest and shoulders. He'd been a force to reckon with before; now he exuded a power and determination far beyond their collective abilities to control.

He commanded instant attention, despite his casual jeans and T-shirt. "Gentlemen," he greeted them congenially enough as he tossed a black leather jacket onto the only vacant chair. "It's been a while."

"Here for a brief visit?" Ben asked hopefully.

Sam flashed the grin that had been the downfall of half the female population on Delacorte Island. "To be honest, I haven't decided yet."

"Get it over with," the sheriff requested abruptly. "There's only one reason you could have asked us three here. It's about that night."

Sam's grin faded. "Yeah. It's about that night."

The mayor stirred, his girth causing his chair to emit a humanlike groan. "Now, boy…"

Sam moved faster than a cornered cottonmouth. One minute he was lounging across the room, the next he was leaning over the mayor's desk, so close the gold skull-and-crossbones earring he wore sneered straight at Pike. "It's Sam. Or Beaumont, if you prefer. But I won't be called 'boy' by you, Mayor. Never again. We clear on that?"

Pike held up his hands. "Sure, sure. Easy…er…Sam. Didn't mean no offense."

"Good." Sam nodded, straightening. "Very good. Shall we get down to business?"

Ben cleared his throat. "We have business, Mr. Beaumont? Or is it Professor?"

Sam's black eyes flashed in genuine amusement. "Doctor. But let's not stand on formalities. After all, it's not a medical degree. My specialty is finances, as I'm sure you've heard."

"Shall we cut to the chase? What do you want from us, Beaumont?" Rolly demanded.

"Just thought I'd clear up a few things so I can enjoy my visit."

The sheriff glared. "What sort of things?"

"I thought I'd assure y'all that I don't plan on starting any trouble while I'm here."

"That's it?" Mayor Pike asked cautiously.

Sam took a seat and stretched his long legs out in front of him. "Absolutely. I mean...getting even can cause so much trouble. It doesn't involve just the responsible parties." His gaze landed on the mayor. "It would involve hurting wives and stirring up the sort of scandals that lose elections."

The color drained from the mayor's face. "You wouldn't!"

Sam lifted a shoulder in an offhand manner. "I told you I wasn't here for trouble." He turned his attention to the sheriff. "Because then I'd have to talk to Mrs. Cross about that hit-and-run driver who put her in the hospital for all those weeks. Never did find the man responsible, did you, Rolly?"

Sheriff Rawling's jaw worked for a minute. "No," he finally managed to say. "Never did."

"Strange. In a community this small, I'd have thought even you could have handled that." Sam glanced at Ben. "Or handled your daughter's problems. Laura, isn't it?"

It was Ben's turn to choke. "How did you—"

"I made it my business to know." He hadn't changed his position, but suddenly there was a dangerous quality to his posture. "I didn't appreciate being on the business end of all those shotguns. But I understood why you chose such a drastic step. What upset me a tad was what happened afterward."

"What happened afterward?" Ben asked uneasily,

glancing in confusion at his companions. "I...I don't understand."

"I mean whichever one of you came after me. Whichever one hit me from behind and then beat the livin' tar out of me. I have to admit, I do bear a bit of a grudge toward him." A deadly light crept into Sam's dark eyes. "Maybe more than a grudge."

Three jaws dropped open. Sheriff Rawling was the first to recover. "We never laid a hand on you!" Ben and the mayor nodded in adamant agreement. "We dumped you at the docks by the first ferry heading north. That's it."

"Interesting, considering I woke up the next day in a gutter on the mainland. I was..." He shrugged. "Let's just say I was a bit of a mess."

"How do you know it was one of us?"

"There were only three of you determined to toss me off-island." His mouth tilted at one corner. "Well...and Annie. But I don't think she was the one whaling away on me. Not quite her style, is it?"

"No, it isn't!" Ben retorted. "So you've come back to get even with the one who beat you, is that it?"

"Not quite." Sam stood and snagged his jacket. "I came back for Annie. I'm just giving you three notice that you're not to interfere again. Because this time I'll fight you. And if that happens, somebody'll get hurt." He paused by the door and lifted a winged brow. "We clear?"

He didn't wait for an answer but walked out, leaving the three men to sit in stunned silence.

Rolly muttered a vicious curse. "What do we do now?"

"Was it you?" Pike demanded. "You always did hate the Beaumonts. Did you go after that boy once we'd gone home?"

"Hell, no," Rolly retorted. "Not to say I wasn't tempted. But I didn't do it."

Ben shot to his feet. "Well, you can't think it's me!"

Pike held up his hands. "Gentlemen, please. This isn't getting us anywhere. The question is…what do we do from here? As far as I'm concerned, it's obvious why he's returned."

"He's returned to ruin us," Ben said. A blush crept into his cheeks. "Well…and to ruin Annie, too."

Rolly sighed. "What we have to decide is…do we give him Annie or do we do the honorable thing and save her again?"

Mayor Pike inclined his head. "That's the question all right. An island this small… Hell, I don't have to tell you boys. This place isn't like any other. A reputation is everything. Years back, you were either a pirate or respectable."

The sheriff scowled. "Beaumonts were always pirates. Still are, as far as I'm concerned."

Ben nodded in reluctant agreement. "And Delacortes were always respectable. Why, Annie Delacorte must have the lily-whitest reputation on the whole island."

"Won't stay that way for long. Not with Beaumont hanging around," Rolly observed.

There was a momentary silence. Then the mayor straightened in his chair, looking distinctly officious. "As far as I can see, we don't have any choice in the matter, regardless of the consequences. Not only is Annie our kindergarten teacher and a shining example to the innocents of our community, but she also came to us for help seven years ago and we're honor bound to help her again. It's our job to keep her reputation intact."

The sheriff nodded glumly. "There's no choice a'tall.

Just wish we weren't getting so blasted old. Playing the Three Musketeers gets downright exhausting.''

Ben closed his eyes. "I wish it didn't mean…"

"Our secrets would have come out eventually," Rolly attempted to console. "Best we do the right thing now."

"It's decided, then?" Mayor Pike asked. "All for one?"

"And one for all," the others chorused.

CHAPTER ONE

ANNIE Delacorte pushed her cart down the spacious aisles of Drake's Supermarket. There was an unusual buzz of conversation for a Wednesday, even though it was mid-July, and people were giving her strange looks. It perked her right up. Maybe she'd finally done something to shock the community. She'd certainly been trying hard enough for the past seven years.

Not that she wanted to completely sully her reputation! Heavens, no. She just wanted to give it an attractive bit of tarnish. Tarnish like the streak of purple she'd added to her blond curls. That way, people wouldn't think quite so badly of her when they found out her secret. Maybe it wouldn't seem quite so shocking. Then they could say, "I wondered about all her crazy antics. Strange for a properly brought-up Delacorte, don't you think? But this explains it. Imagine her father protecting the girl from the scandal all this time. I'm not sure *I'd* have been so noble."

A clutch of women cackled softly over bins of onions and potatoes, and ever so casually Annie wheeled her cart in that direction. She paused, pretending to study an attractive pyramid of ruby-red grapefruit. Not that she was eavesdropping. Goodness, no! Saint Annie would never commit such a transgression. Her mouth curved downward. If they only knew!

She inched closer.

"...back. My Bertie saw it with his own two eyes,"

Rosie Hinkle was saying. "And Sheriff Rolly confirmed it."

"No! Not after all these years." A delighted twitter escaped one woman in the clutch. "The nerve of the boy."

The nerve of what boy? *Who*? One of her students? Annie sighed in frustration. If only she'd gotten here a few minutes earlier, she'd know.

"He's back, I tell you. My Bertie doesn't lie."

"Well...not since he was eleven," said another. "He's been a good boy ever since Sheriff Rolly gave him that talking-to. But if Bertie says it's so, that's good enough for me."

Darn it all! *Who's* back? What *he*? If only she'd hustled right over. She could have looked desperate to lay hands on a grapefruit instead of interested in the latest gossip. She leaned closer under the pretext of snatching up a particularly plump fruit in desperate need of a thorough examination. Though what there was to examine on a grapefruit was a bit hard to imagine. One pretty much looked like the next. She gave it a squeeze and a sniff anyway.

"Well, what does he want? Why has he come?"

Bertie's mother glanced left and right. "I'll tell you, but you have to promise not to let another living soul know what I'm about to say." The hens, as they were affectionately called by the islanders, all nodded eagerly. "My Bertie had it straight from Sheriff Rolly. And the sheriff had it straight from the devil himself. Can you imagine the gall of the man?"

There was a significant pause, and Annie reached for another grapefruit that was a bit closer to the huddle of women, allowing her to sidle nearer.

"Sam Beaumont's come back for revenge. He told

Rolly, Ben and the mayor that he's going to ruin our sweet Annie for what she did to him. Can you imagine? It would be the first time a Delacorte ever had her reputation destroyed. And at the hands of a Beaumont, no less."

Annie jerked in surprise, bumping the bottom of the pyramid. The pile wobbled precariously, then a grapefruit popped loose. A waterfall of ruby reds cascaded onto the floor, bouncing in every direction like bright yellow beach balls. She stood stock-still and ankle-deep in grapefruit, the focus of all eyes.

"Oh, my," Rosie Hinkle said. "Annie, dear, I didn't mean for you to hear about—"

Gracefully plowing through the mess, Annie announced in her best schoolteacher's voice, "Cleanup on aisle two, Tommy. Ladies," she said with a gracious nod as she swept past, kicking citrus from her path.

Before she could make good her escape, Ben Drake gave chase. "Annie! Annie, I need to speak to you right away."

"I heard. Sam Beaumont's in town." She edged toward the exit, fighting the urge to break and run. "Don't worry. Despite what some may think—" she gave the hens her most intimidating scowl, which wasn't terribly intimidating when a body was only five foot four and looked like one of those sugar-sweet princesses in a Disney movie—at least, that was how her kindergartners had described her "—he's not after me."

"I think we should discuss this in private," Ben insisted. "There are *things* you don't know."

Discuss Sam Beaumont privately? Had Ben lost his ever blessed mind? Not a chance. She had to get out of Drake's while she could still hide the wild exhilaration humming through her veins—an exhilaration coupled with sheer panic. "No need. I have to run. Aunt Myrtle is waiting."

"Annie…"

Lifting a hand in farewell, she darted from the store. In the parking lot, she hastened over to her Harley and climbed aboard, kicking it into gear. Tucking her skirt carefully around her legs and plopping a helmet on top of her blond curls—after all, one couldn't be *too* outrageous—she zipped out of the lot and turned toward home.

Sam Beaumont was back! Good golly, Miss Molly, what was she going to do? Because if "that wild Beaumont boy" as he'd been dubbed at the ripe age of four had returned to Delacorte Island, it could only be for one purpose. The hens had it half-right. He hadn't returned to ruin her—at least, not the way they meant. Heck, anywhere else on earth, a tattered reputation wouldn't cause so much as a puckered brow. But Sam *had* returned to get even with those who'd driven him from his home. And the one thing he'd most want to wreak revenge upon was her all-too-guilty head.

She increased her speed well past the posted limit, her hair flying behind her in a long, sunlit stream. Whipping through town, she passed Rosie Hinkle's son, Bertie, who also happened to be the local deputy and her brother-in-law. He lifted his hand in greeting, a gesture she automatically returned. She didn't even bother glancing in her side mirror to see if he intended to ticket her for speeding. He'd laugh himself silly at the mere suggestion. Just as Sam Beaumont could do no right, Annie Delacorte of Delacorte Island could do no wrong—no matter how hard she tried. Her chin wobbled precariously. If they only knew.

Turning down a dirt lane, she avoided potholes with

practiced ease, as well as a king snake, an angry gray squirrel and a pair of courting doves. Roaring up to the doorway, she cut the engine and set the kickstand. Ripping off her helmet, she allowed it to drop to the sand as she ran up the worn planks leading to Aunt Myrtle's porch. She should go in through the kitchen door. Everyone did. But today she was in too much of a hurry. Allowing a few mosquitoes and a bit of sand into the front foyer was less important than getting the latest news to Aunt Myrtle. Even so, she took a second to kick off her sandals and brush her feet before entering, scolded all the while for her impertinence by the Carolina wren nesting in a nearby flower basket.

"He's back!" she shouted the instant the door banged shut behind her. "It's all over town." Pelting down the hallway, she careered off the wall and darted into the kitchen. "And guess what that silly woman Rosie Hinkle says he wants?"

"How about my old motorcycle for starters?"

Annie skidded to a halt. Dammit all. She should have anticipated this and hadn't. "Dang."

Instead of Aunt Myrtle, Sam Beaumont lounged at the table. "Interesting that my bike ended up in your possession." He tilted his chair onto two legs. "Next time I get thrown off the island, I'm going to have to insist they toss my Harley off with me."

"I'll be sure to make a note of it," she replied with more composure than common sense.

His eyes glittered a warning, a warning she'd be smart to heed. "You do that."

A dainty cup of hot tea steamed in front of him, a semitransparent wheel of lemon floating on top. The sight of this feminine delicacy coupled with such blatant power should have looked incongruous. Instead, it only served to emphasize the sheer masculinity of the man.

He was dressed all in black—a T-shirt that clung to every sculpted muscle, black jeans that outlined lean, strong thighs and black boots. The color mirrored his pitch-colored Beaumont eyes and hair. Thick curls tumbled in careless abandon across his brow, emphasizing those wicked, wicked eyes. A descendant of pirates, he was perfectly suited to the role, particularly with the skull-and-crossbones earring he'd worn for more years than she could recall. Lord help her, but she'd missed him.

Annie glanced around uneasily. "Where's Aunt Myrtle?"

"Upstairs, talking on the phone. About me, if I'm not mistaken." His chair banged down onto all four legs and he slowly climbed to his feet. "Whatever are you doing here, Miss Delacorte? This is Beaumont land in case you've forgotten."

"Didn't Aunt Myrtle mention?" Annie asked as casually as she could manage. "I live here now."

His eyes narrowed as he approached. "Since when?"

She shrugged, wishing she could avoid his compelling gaze but unable to. "Not long after you left. She needed a live-in companion and I wanted to leave the nest. It was a perfect match."

He took a moment to digest the information. "I'm surprised old man Delacorte let you anywhere near a living, breathing Beaumont."

"Don't be ridiculous," she retorted, taking instant umbrage. "It wasn't all Beaumonts Pops objected to."

"Just me." He allowed the dry observation to settle uncomfortably between them before asking, "You still haven't answered my question. What are you doing here?''

He wasn't going to let the subject drop, she realized apprehensively. That could be a problem. Once Sam latched onto something, he didn't let go until physically forced to back off. Somehow she doubted there was anyone willing—or able—to force Sam to do anything he wasn't already inclined to do. Not this time. "I told you. I live here now. As for Pops...I didn't ask. I just did it."

"Defied your father? You, Annie?" Sam shook his head in patent disbelief. "Hard to imagine, all things considered."

Had she really been such a pushover? Perhaps that's how most perceived her—as the good, dutiful daughter. Little did they know. "Well, believe it. Because it happened. I'm here and I'm staying put."

To her relief, Sam lifted a shoulder in dismissal, apparently satisfied. "So what happened to your place?" he asked.

"Pansy and Bertie live there now. They married and moved in not long after Pops died."

He lifted an eyebrow. "What about the beach house your grandmother gave you? I would have thought you'd want to live there instead of imposing on Myrtle."

"I'm not imposing." She drew a calming breath. "As for the beach house...I sold it."

His frown deepened. For some reason, that tiny admission managed to annoy him more than anything else she'd said so far, though she couldn't imagine why. "You sold it? Delacorte land? What the hell were you thinking?"

Annie planted her hands on her hips. "You know what? I don't have to answer your questions. I don't have to answer *anybody's* questions. It was just a house and land and now it's someone else's house and land.''

''And after you sold out, you moved in with my aunt Myrtle?''

Sold out? Is that how he regarded her actions? She suppressed the momentary hurt. One of these days she'd have to toughen up and stop being so darned sensitive, particularly when it came to a certain dangerously attractive Beaumont. It was her land and she could do what she pleased. As for Aunt Myrtle... ''She's not *your* aunt Myrtle. She belongs to everybody,'' Annie clarified. ''She's only a distant connection of yours. *Very* distant.'' It seemed vital to stress that point.

He didn't take kindly to the reminder. ''Aunt Myrtle raised me from the time I was ten. I think that gives me prior claim.''

''Maybe it would, if you hadn't left.''

''Left?'' His bark of laughter was downright chilling. ''I didn't leave. I was thrown off the island, remember?''

It took every ounce of self-restraint not to turn tail and run. But if she'd learned one thing about dealing with Sam, it was to stand her ground and come out swinging. He'd taught her that the day he'd crashed her sixth birthday party. ''I haven't forgotten a thing.''

''Neither have I.'' He snagged her around the waist and hauled her up against him. ''Well, Annie? Aren't you going to welcome me home?''

She shoved at his shoulders, not that it did any good. He was as uncontrollable as a storm-driven breaker and twice as relentless. It left two options—to ride him out or to be swept along. ''Aside from Aunt Myrtle, I'm probably the only one who will,'' she informed him tartly.

"If that's a welcome, it's a mite lacking. I know you can do better."

He didn't wait for her to come up with any brilliant—let alone safe—ideas, like a handshake or impersonal hug. Instead, he took what he wanted. And what he wanted was a kiss that was the most passionate she'd ever experienced in all of her twenty-five years.

How could she have forgotten what his lips felt like? How they tasted? How with one hungry touch he overwhelmed every sense, particularly her common sense? At eighteen, she hadn't stood a chance against his raw masculinity. She'd been shaken and confused by the deep well of desire he'd tapped with such ease, the unbearable hankering he'd stirred, yet never quite satisfied.

Now, she knew precisely what those feelings were...and where they'd lead. She also discovered something she'd been too innocent to realize before. It wasn't one-sided. His arousal ran every bit as deep and strong as her own. He was just better at hiding it; better yet at hiding what drove his actions. While she found him impossible to resist, still cared for him on an emotional plane as well as a physical one, he remained unreadable. He was as closed to her today as he'd been all those years ago.

Eventually, she'd have to confront him, find out what he really wanted from her. But right now she didn't care. His mouth fitted so deliciously over hers, the taste as intoxicating as wild berries, sun ripened to juicy perfection. He cupped her face, his thumbs massaging the tense muscles of her jaw. She relaxed, no doubt as he'd intended, her lips parting to allow him entry. Dear heaven, but he was good at this. Gentle yet firm, a fierce passion bridled by unmistakable tenderness. Dusty memories were replaced with bittersweet reality, half-forgotten dreams resurrected with each thrust and nip, reminding her with heartbreaking deliberation of all she'd given up when she drove him away.

She could lose herself in this man. Lose her sanity, her self-restraint and her reputation as a "good" girl. She'd wanted to taint her image a little. No doubt Sam would be happy to oblige. Not that she'd allow that to happen. There was too much at stake, too many people who'd be hurt if she gave in to the one thing she craved most in all the world. Fighting for strength, she wriggled from his arms. To her surprise, not to mention a wee bit of disappointment, he let her go without a struggle.

They stared at each other across the width of the kitchen. To Annie's relief, she wasn't the only one fighting for breath. It would have been too galling if she was, especially since he'd managed to imprint himself on every one of her senses. His taste was stamped on her mouth and his scent filled her lungs. Even the power of his arms was a lingering warmth on her back. He'd always been like that—a force to be reckoned with, creating as strong an impact as the hurricanes that periodically battered their small island.

Finally gathering her wits, she shot off the first volley. "Not only do you look like a damned pirate, you act like one, too."

Acknowledging her swift recovery, he saluted her with a grin. "A schoolteacher shouldn't use language like that."

"You always did bring out the worst in me," she complained.

"Really? That's not how I see it." His black eyes held a knowing gleam that caused warmth to blossom in her cheeks. "I'd say I brought out the best you had to offer.

I wonder how everyone would react if they knew you'd given me such an enthusiastic welcome?''

"Tell them! Tell every last one of them." She folded her arms across her chest. "They wouldn't believe you, more's the pity." Perhaps if she'd had a reputation like Sam's mother, they'd have believed the worst. Poor woman.

His expression turned grim. "No, they wouldn't."

Since his humor had faded, this might be a good time to address some of the stickier issues remaining between them. She took a deep breath, praying for strength. This was going to hurt. "So why *did* you come back, Sam?"

"I thought you already knew the answer to that."

"I know what everyone's saying." She forced herself to hold his gaze, to absorb the impact of those Beaumont eyes. "Now I'd like to hear it from you."

The change in him was instantaneous. Gone was the lazily amused man she'd loved so long ago. And in his place stood a hardened stranger. "And what precisely have you been told?"

"Oh, gosh. The list is endless. Let's see...." She ticked off on her fingers. "You've come to pick up the motorcycle you left behind. You're on the island to cause trouble. You're here to get revenge by ruining me. You're visiting old friends and checking up on your property. You know." She tried for a nonchalant shrug. "The usual sort of stuff most people who've been away for a spell come back to do."

For a moment, she thought she'd successfully slipped her ruination past him. She should have known better. One black brow hitched upward. "Wait a sec. What was that middle one?"

She widened her eyes and tried for an innocent expression. "Which one? Visiting old friends?"

He gave her a look of dry amusement. "No, not that one."

"Umm…" She scuffed her sandy toe against the linoleum. It was a big mistake. The childhood habit had always given her away the few times she'd tried to varnish the truth. And Sam knew it, darn him. "You're here to cause trouble?"

Amusement still flickered in his gaze. "Not that, either."

"Oh." She cleared her throat. "Maybe it was the 'you're here to get revenge by ruining me' one."

"Bingo."

She made a dismissive gesture. "You know how crazy gossip can get. It's not like anyone actually believes it or anything."

"Ruining you." To her dismay, he seemed to savor the words. "How Victorian. Now where in the world did that come from?"

"Rosie Hinkle got it direct from Bertie. And Bertie got it straight from Sheriff Rolly."

"Right from the horse's mouth, huh? And here I always thought he resembled the other end."

"Have you come back to ruin me?" she couldn't help asking. Good grief! She sounded almost hopeful. "Is that why you're here?"

"What do you think?"

To be honest, she hadn't had time to think. Thirty short minutes ago, Sam had been a distant memory, one she'd only savored in the quiet solitude of sleepless nights, when her resistance had been low and the hurt running high. "I think it's been seven years since our…relationship ended—"

"Damn, but you've gotten good at whitewashing history," he marveled.

"*And* that's given you ample opportunity to get over the slight to your pride. Now that you've made your mark in the financial community—what did they call you? The Beaumont Bull?"

"You're ducking the issue."

"I'm sure you've come to check up on—" she waved her hand airily "—*things.*"

"Good try. But wrong."

If she'd been one of her students, she'd have stamped her foot. "Darn it, Sam! Why are you really here? Why now?"

"I've come home to take care of unfinished business. What's so strange about that?"

Unfinished business? Aside from getting even with her and the men who'd chased him off, there was only one other piece of unfinished business he'd need to take care of. Understanding hit like a force five hurricane. "Oh, no," she said with all the ferocity of a lioness protecting her cub. "You can't have her. She's mine now."

"What the *hell* are you talking about?"

"Aunt Myrtle. You left her behind and that gives me squatter's rights. You can't just sweep into town and take her away from me." His eyes narrowed as he analyzed her declaration. Apparently, her vehemence had given her away. When would she learn? She'd have to be more careful around Sam.

"I'm not planning on taking Myrtle anywhere," he replied mildly enough. "Although I'd be happy to take her off your hands any time you want."

"No! You left and I'm keeping her."

"Left?"

Oops. She stumbled back as he started toward her. "You know what I mean."

"Oh, I know." His tone bit deep, resonating with years

of remembered anger and hostility. "I know you said you loved me. I know you promised to leave the island on your eighteenth birthday and marry me. And I also know what happened next, on what should have been my wedding day."

Every word he uttered was sheer agony. "Don't, Sam—"

"What's the matter, Annie? Is this too much for your delicate Delacorte ears? Tough. I was the one stuck living through what you set in motion."

"I never meant—"

He cut her off with an abrupt gesture. "Never meant what? For the town's leading citizens to line up on my doorstep with half a dozen shotguns ready to blast chunks out of my hide? Well, relax. They rethought that plan once I explained my objections."

It took a moment for her to grasp what he meant. "You *fought* them? Men with shotguns?"

"I stated my objections," he repeated dryly. "In as physical a manner as they'd allow. It was enough to convince them to back off. Instead of shooting me, they simply tied me up, tossed me into the bed of a pickup and drove for the ferry docks." A taut muscle spasmed along his jawline. "Too bad you missed it, sweetheart. If you'd come along for the party, you could have watched them dump me there like so much garbage."

"I'm sorry, Sam—"

"Sorry?" The word slipped softly between them, rumbling with the turbulence of emotions too painful to openly acknowledge. "That's it? 'Sorry, Sam. I changed my mind and was too much of a coward to tell you?'"

"Yes." He ripped a chair from his path and she flinched. "I was a coward. Okay? Is that what you want to hear?"

"It's a start. But let's see what other confessions I can pry loose." His unrelenting approach backed her toward the counter. "What else is there, Annie? You were such a coward you sent a posse after me instead of confronting me directly. Now why is that? Were you afraid of me?"

"*No!*" Not Sam. Never Sam. "I was young and foolish and hoped to avoid an argument. Satisfied?"

"Not even close." He stopped inches away, so near the shadow of his beard filled her gaze while the harsh intake of his breath resonated in her ears. "And because you couldn't face an argument, you routed Ben Drake, Rolly and Mayor Pike from their beds to handle the situation. You sent a posse to do the talking for you. Is that how it went down?"

She swallowed, the bitterness of regrets like acid on her tongue. "Something like that."

"Let me guess. The shotguns were punctuation, right?"

She wouldn't cry. She wouldn't! She focused every scrap of attention on the wall behind him. There was a plaster casting of her hand hanging there, one of the few personal belongings she'd brought from home when she'd moved in with Aunt Myrtle. She'd been in kindergarten when the mold was made. Beside her tiny handprint hung an identical one Sam had done several years before her own. It was larger, the hand slammed into the mold with all the strength and enthusiasm a five-year-old could muster. Hardened plaster curled like waves away from the deep wells left by his fingers and palm. He had that effect on life even then—driving through it, forcing all in his path to give way.

Sam shifted his stance, blocking her view of the wall. "Where have you gone, Annie?"

"Away," she answered simply. To a time Sam had

filled her world and been the love of her life. A time she'd been secure in the knowledge that one day she'd marry him and bear his children, children whose handprints would decorate their walls, as well.

A time that would never be.

"You can't escape me that easily. I have questions. Lots of questions. And you'll answer every last one of them."

She folded her arms across her chest. "What's the point? It happened. It's over and done with. Talking about it isn't going to change a blessed thing."

"I wasn't planning to waste time talking. You might remember I preferred action."

She turned on him. "I won't let you do it, Sam!"

"What? Have my revenge?"

"Well, that, too. But I meant Aunt Myrtle."

"How did you get from revenge to Aunt Myrtle?"

She faced him down, practically daring him to do his worst. "Because I don't believe for one little minute you came back for me."

An odd expression crept into his gaze. "No?"

"Why would you? Because I had you helped off the island? That's not much of a reason."

It was the wrong thing to say. Again. "*Helped* off? You have an interesting way with words, sweetheart. We're going to have to work on that."

"Children, children," Aunt Myrtle chided from the doorway. "You're not arguing, are you?"

"No, ma'am," Annie instantly replied. Old habits, it would seem, died hard.

Aunt Myrtle carried sixty years on her spare frame and looked every single day of her age with a few heaped on just to prove that life wasn't always fair to the kindhearted. A difficult youth and a serious car accident while in her thirties had aged her unbearably. Yet she still maintained her sense of humor, along with a graciousness and bone-deep kindness that made her one of the most beloved women on the island. Here was the true saint. Next to her, Annie was merely a pretender to the throne. She shot Sam a warning glance. She'd cut out her tongue sooner than say anything upsetting. Judging by Sam's expression, he felt the same way.

Aunt Myrtle carefully tapped her way into the kitchen, the cane Annie had bought her as a birthday present topped by a beautifully carved bird of paradise. "I see you're welcoming Sam home, Annie. Isn't this a lovely surprise?"

"Lovely." And actually, it was. She might have had Sam run off all those years ago, but her feelings for him had never died. And now…seeing him again, seeing the subtle changes seven years had wrought…tasting his kisses…

"You'll be staying with me, of course?" Aunt Myrtle invited Sam, giving him a fierce hug and kiss.

He nodded, helping her into a chair. "Thanks, I'd appreciate it. I also wanted to check out the old place. See how much of it's fallen apart. Maybe do some repairs."

"It's a mess," Annie volunteered. "The hurricanes haven't helped."

Myrtle nodded, smiling her appreciation for the cup of tea Sam poured. "Thank you, dear. But you did know Annie goes over every now and then to tidy the place and arrange for the worst of the damage to be repaired, didn't you?"

That caught his attention. "Has she?"

Annie shrugged. "I always figured you'd return. Besides, I…I owed you."

"And now it's payback time."

Myrtle clucked her tongue. "My, my. That sounds so ominous, Sam. You run around saying things like that and you'll set people to talking."

"He already has," Annie acknowledged.

"That's because they have nothing better to do with themselves," Myrtle said serenely. "And Sam does nothing to counter their unfortunate opinions. That will change once he's been here a while."

"Don't count on it, sweetheart." He pinched Myrtle's cheek, giving her a roguish smile. "I was always good fodder for gossip."

"You were a tad unruly," she confessed. But her love came through in the softness of her deep-set eyes and the brilliance of her smile. "It comes from being a Beaumont, dear heart."

"Well, since I'm obligated to give people something to talk about, I'd better get to it." He switched his attention to Annie. "Why don't you come with me? You can show me what you've done to the place while I was gone."

She gave him a cocky grin. "Your motorcycle or mine?"

"Same thing, isn't it?" He frowned. "Now that I think about it, you've gotten damned possessive of my belongings. My old motorcycle, my aunt, my house. I wonder why?"

Aunt Myrtle answered before Annie had a chance. "I think you should look into that, Sam. In fact, I think you should investigate the matter very carefully."

"Trust me. I will." He glanced at Annie. "Coming?"

This was a bad idea…an irresistibly bad idea. "Should I have Aunt Myrtle chaperon us?"

He shrugged. "That's up to you."

"Well, are you going to try anything while we're at your house?" she demanded.

"I'm sure going to give it my best effort."

"Now, Sam. I thought I taught you better than that," Aunt Myrtle reprimanded sternly.

He sighed. "Yes, ma'am. I believe you did."

"Always give it your best effort." She took a dainty sip of tea before adding, "But in the end, make sure the deed gets done."

There was a moment of absolute silence. Annie stared in disbelief. If she didn't know better, she'd swear Aunt Myrtle was trying to encourage him.

Then Sam chuckled. "Yes, *ma'am*," he assured her, sweeping a protesting Annie toward the door. "Heaven knows, I wouldn't want to disappoint you."

Aunt Myrtle indulged in a smile as the two disappeared through the door. "That's what I'm counting on. Yes, indeed, I am."

CHAPTER TWO

SAM guided his Harley along a path through the woods from Aunt Myrtle's to his place. Annie had climbed on behind him without a murmur of protest and now she clung, just like old times. Her arms circled his waist, her fists digging into the flat of his belly while her slender thighs cupped his hips.

Instead of finding pleasure in the contact, it left him cursing every rut and hole they had the misfortune to encounter, because with each tiny bounce her soft breasts scraped against his back. And heaven forbid the tires slide on sand, because whenever that happened, she'd wriggle her bottom into position again, cradling him closer than before.

The dual action drove him wild with desire. What would she do if he overturned the bike and rolled her up against the nearest sand dune? Would she spread those sweet thighs in welcome or shriek like an outraged spinster? He didn't bother to find out. Deciding discretion was the better part of retaining his sanity, he gunned the engine and swept recklessly up the dirt drive.

The house he'd inherited from his parents was located on the sound, facing west, like all Beaumont land. Oceanfront property had traditionally been owned by Delacortes, and borne the brunt of storms and winds and pounding surf. But his place, called Soundings, located on an undeveloped peninsula and surrounded by wetlands, commanded a spectacular view of the calmer waters between the island and the mainland. It also had the added benefit of several sweeping decks from which he and Annie had frequently watched the sunset—when they could slip away from her father.

"Sorry about the lawn," Annie said as they climbed off his motorcycle. "I meant to have someone come out and mow it down a bit."

He broke away from her, fighting to hide how badly she'd affected him. Hell, it was worse than when he'd been a randy teenager. The loss of control filled him with an ironic amusement that did little to ease his frustration but helped immensely to restore his sense of humor. "Mowing my lawn wasn't your responsibility."

She shrugged. "I decided it was."

Curious. "Now why would you think that?"

"It's how I was raised."

The reminder irritated him. "That's right. You're a Delacorte." He waited a beat before adding, "As high-handed as they come...and one of the last of a dying breed. Or is it *the* last now that your sisters have married?"

She rose instantly to the bait. Swiveling to face him, her mouth compressed into a tight line and her chin jutted as defiantly as a Beaumont. If it weren't for the Delacorte coloring and dainty stature, he'd have thought her a kissing cousin—the relationship close enough to be considered kin, but distant enough to marry without worrying about three-eyed offspring.

"A dying breed," she repeated. "You can't resist rubbing that in, can you?"

It was his turn to shrug. "Why not? It's not my fault the Delacortes can't plow a fertile field. The Beaumonts have always been prolific and proud of it. Hell, I have more relatives across the eastern seaboard than I can count. I even have a cousin somewhere in Costa Rica."

He frowned in contemplation. "Or is it Nevada? Maybe both. I seem to recall he goes back and forth between his coffee plantation and his wife's place."

He'd managed to distract her with that one. "That's your cousin Rafe, isn't it? I hadn't heard he'd married."

"Hitched himself to some crazy woman who spends most of her spare time planning marriage balls."

"Marriage balls?" she asked, clearly intrigued. "What are those?"

"They're a big bash designed to bring people together who want to find a partner. They meet, then wed and bed, all in one night." Sam shrugged, allowing cynicism to slash through his tone. "Apparently, some people in this world actually want to get married. Go figure."

His comment hit the mark. Her baby blues widened a fraction, mirroring an anguish that struck like a blow. When would he learn? Annie's pain had always been his own, magnified by some quirk of fate.

He released his breath in a gusty sigh. "Aw, hell, honey. I'm sorry."

"Forget it. I deserved it." Her voice dropped. "I deserve that and more."

"Why?" The question was torn from him and he clenched his hands so he wouldn't touch her. If he took her in his arms again, she wouldn't escape. He'd drop her to the overgrown grass and make her his in the most permanent way possible. "Can't you just tell me that much?"

For an instant, he thought she'd reply. Then she turned abruptly and faced the house. "We'd better get on with this. Aunt Myrtle will wonder what's taking so long. And there's been enough speculation on that point, don't you think?" She didn't wait for a response but pointed to the roof on the north side. "You had some damage there. A tree came down on it during Hurricane Bonnie."

It took a full minute for him to release his anger and regain a small measure of calm. "Let's go in and take a look."

She silently followed as he climbed the porch steps and shoved open the front door. "All the doors and casings have warped over the years," she warned. "They'll need to be trimmed up and rehung. I guess you can take care of it easily enough if you're staying. Of course, you'll also need to have the power turned on. The water, too. But that shouldn't take much more than a day or two to arrange."

He gave a noncommittal response, knowing full well it wasn't what she wanted to hear. He still hadn't answered that all-important question. Was he sticking around? Or had he returned for a short visit—just long enough to take his revenge before returning to Wall Street? Since he didn't know the answer to that himself, it was a bit difficult to satisfy her curiosity.

He waited a minute for his eyes to adjust to the dim interior, then examined the foyer in surprise. "Looks clean."

"I stir myself every so often to come in and give the place a good going-over."

"That must set people to talking." He rocked back on his heels, slanting her an amused glance. "Or is that only to be expected of Saint Annie?"

She shoved her hands into the pockets of her sundress...but not before he'd seen them clench in white-knuckled fists. Interesting that she resisted the label others on the island would be only too happy to accept. "I can't help what people think," she informed him. "I don't come over here to please them."

Then why did she? "We had some good times here. Do you think about that when you drop by?"

He must have hit another nerve. She walked determinedly toward the staircase, carefully avoiding his gaze. "Why don't we go to the attic first so you can check out the damage up there?"

She didn't wait for him to respond but started up the steps. Temptation beckoned and he followed, admiring the graceful sway of her pert backside and the jaunty bounce of sunlit curls tumbling down the length of her spine. Her dress molded briefly to long, slender legs and thighs, teasing him with a glimpse of what was hidden beneath before billowing modestly outward. He found it ironic that a simple calf-length sundress could stir a more potent reaction than the slinky bits of nothing commonly worn by the women he dated.

The final stairs leading from the second story to the attic were narrow and steep, and it was hotter than Hades in the cramped area beneath the rafters. One side had been boarded over, the tiny square window sealed in plastic. She crossed to the opposite end, to the only other window, and tried to force it open.

When she didn't succeed, Sam came up behind, no doubt crowding her if the rigid line of her spine was any indication. "Here. Let me."

She stepped aside, though probably not as far as she'd like, since the steep pitch of the roof prevented her from entirely escaping physical contact. Her hair clung to the nape of her neck in damp ringlets and the upper slopes of her breasts glowed with the soft sheen of perspiration. She smelled of summer warmth and salt-tainted earth underscored by a delicate woman's fragrance. It was a unique scent he knew well, one he'd carried in the deep recesses of his memory for seven long years.

Giving the casing a hard whack, he forced the swollen wood to give way. The window swung open and a soft breath of humidity-laden air swept into the stuffy interior. Annie closed her eyes and tilted back her head, easing the loosened bodice of her dress away from her chest. The sultry breeze kissed the dew from her skin, while sunlight slipped through the bodice of her dress, turning it almost transparent. He caught tantalizing glimpses of her sweetly rounded breasts, the rosy centers a delicate blush of color against the thin cotton barrier. Sam could only stare, certain he'd carry the image of this moment for the rest of his life.

Slowly, her lashes drifted upward, her eyes shadowed within the dusky gloom of the attic—shadowed, too, by memories still ripe enough to add sweetness to the bitter tang of a love long lost. For an instant, her lips parted as though hungering for another kiss. It would be so easy to draw her into his arms, to give her the physical surcease she craved. But he didn't want to win that way. He wanted more. He wanted it all. Body *and* soul. Only when she surrendered emotionally as well as physically would he be appeased.

"What did you have to show me, Annie?"

Her breath hitched in the heavy air, awareness swift to return. She released the neckline of her dress and pressed her hand protectively to the exposed cleft between her breasts. It was such an utterly feminine gesture, one made by countless women through the ages when confronted by a masculine threat. He didn't know whether to be amused, insulted or reassured. He caught her fingers in his and drew them away from her body. He could hear the frantic give and take of her breath, see the rapid rise and fall of her breasts. It would be so easy to take the next step.

Annie was ripe for ruining.

Instead, he gestured toward the part of the roof that had been damaged. ''I gather you had someone board it up.''

Her swift recovery impressed the hell out of him. Murmuring something painfully polite, she eluded his grasp and strode to the opposite end of the attic. No doubt she confronted her students with similar poise—her chin high, her step brisk and purposeful, her gaze direct and determined. Only her glorious blond hair escaped her mastery, tumbling merrily in utter disorder. It made her infinitely more human, more vulnerable...and appealingly flawed.

''The repairs were makeshift,'' she explained in her best schoolteacher tone of voice. Sam buried a smile. He'd give her credit for trying, but there wasn't a schoolteacher alive who'd succeeded in intimidating him. Perhaps Annie would be the first. She had a good shot at it, particularly when she leveled her best ''Aunt Myrtle'' look on him. ''Are you listening?''

''Hanging on every word,'' he assured her gravely.

Satisfied, her arm swung in a wide arc to indicate a good portion of the roof. ''So you'll probably need to replace this whole section. You might also want to check for dry rot and termites. I've chased the squirrels and bats out.'' She glanced over her shoulder, the corners of her eyes crinkling in amusement. ''Good golly, was that ever a mess.''

Her soft chuckle provoked a smile. He never could resist her laughter. ''Yeah, I can imagine.'' Crossing to inspect the damage, he took care not to crowd her again. Scaring her off wasn't part of the plan. ''You did good, sweetheart. Thanks.''

"This is the worst of it. You did get a bit of flooding in the kitchen, so I ripped up the linoleum."

"I assume I'll need to replace the floorboards?"

"They're pretty warped," she conceded. "But you could always tell people it adds character to the place if you'd rather not go to the expense of fixing them."

"Cute. Should I also tell them whose idea it was?"

"Feel free," she offered magnanimously. "I'm sure that'll go a long way toward convincing people."

"Saint Annie strikes again?"

A reluctant smile drifted across her mouth. "It can come in handy. Sometimes." But not often, he read between the lines. She started plucking at her neckline, fanning herself in an effort to relieve the oppressive heat.

Enough was enough. He could take it from here. "Come on. You're sweltering. Let's go downstairs."

After closing the window, they trooped to the second story. Annie paused in the hallway. "Oh! I just thought of something else you should see." She sidetracked into the bedroom directly beneath the damaged portion of the roof and attic. Chunks of ceiling plaster had fallen, leaving gaping holes overhead, while wallpaper curled toward the floor along one whole wall. "This will need immediate attention, too."

Once again, she crossed to the nearest window. This one opened with ease. The screen meant to keep out mosquitoes and other flying menaces had long since shredded in seven years' worth of nor'easters and tropical storms. A brisker breeze than the one in the attic swept through the room and Annie propped a hip in the open window, sighing in pleasure.

"I always did love the views from here."

At one point he'd thought they'd have a lifetime together to appreciate all Soundings had to offer. That particular dream had died a hard death. "You'd have enjoyed the place more if your father hadn't declared it taboo. I can't count the number of times he came roaring up the drive to drag you off home."

Mischief glimmered in her eyes. "Which only encouraged me to come here at every opportunity."

His jaw clenched. "I shouldn't have let you. You were too young."

"I was safe with you."

It was the wrong thing to say and her stricken expression acknowledged that fact. As though to underscore it, a gusty breeze caught the bedroom door and slammed it shut with an earsplitting bang. For an instant, neither of them moved. Then Annie scrambled to her feet and hastened to the door, grabbing at the diamond-cut glass knob.

"I don't believe this," she muttered.

With a long-suffering sigh, Sam joined her. "What's wrong now?"

She turned the knob rapidly back and forth, then shook it. "It won't open."

"It's probably warped like every other window and door in the place. Let me try."

"I can get it!" She attacked the knob with unmistakable ferocity, then froze. "Damn, damn, damn."

"Now what?"

Slowly, she turned to face him, offering up the knob and part of the assembly. "I think I broke it."

"I think you're right." He took the knob and eased her to one side. Stooping, he peered at the mechanism. If he were careful, he might be able to slip everything together without the hardware on the other side falling out. If he were very, very— A muffled clang sounded in the hallway.

"What happened?"

He straightened. "You broke the door."

"Can't you fix it?" A thread of panic sounded in her voice. "You're good at that sort of stuff, aren't you?"

"I excel at finances. I'm okay at fixing stuff. And I downright stink at reaching through a one-inch-diameter hole and picking up a doorknob that's rolled halfway across the hall."

"Can't you break down the door?"

Hell, she really was desperate. "Only if it's half-eaten through by termites or dry rot." He tested it with his shoulder. "Which this one apparently isn't."

"So what do we do now?"

"I don't know about you, but I intend to make myself comfortable until we're rescued."

The only two pieces of furniture in the room were a bed and a rickety chair. He chose the bed. Propping himself against the headboard, he waited to see what she'd do next. She fluttered uselessly around the door for a few minutes, stooping to peek through the hole for the knob before pounding on the solid wooden panel. Eventually, she realized the utter futility of her actions and crossed to the chair, lowering herself gingerly onto it. To his disappointment, it held. If it hadn't, he might have talked her into joining him on the bed. Maybe.

"How long do you think it'll be until someone comes?" she asked uneasily.

"Depends on Aunt Myrtle. How long do you suppose it'll take before she gets worried?"

"Days."

He chuckled at her forlorn response. "In that case, it looks like you and I will have ample time to share this bed." For some strange reason, that thoroughly alarmed her. She leaped to her feet and gave the door another try.

"Calm down, Annie. I was only joking. I'll tell you what. Why don't we just relax and talk a spell?"

Her hand crept to the bodice of her dress again, the fingers splayed protectively across her chest. "About what?" she asked uneasily.

"Tell me about your two sisters. You said Pansy and Bertie got married?"

It worked like a charm. She returned to the chair and sat on the very edge of the seat, hands folded primly and ankles crossed. "I'm sure Aunt Myrtle must have kept you updated about everyone."

"In all honesty, we avoided reference to the Delacortes."

She winced. "Of course. Let's see…Pansy married Bertie Hinkle the year Pops died."

"That wasn't long after I left. Had she even graduated high school?"

"The day before. She and Bertie married on her eighteenth birthday." For an instant, Sam thought her mouth trembled. But perhaps he'd imagined it, since when he looked again, her chin was set at an aggressive angle that belied any hint of emotion. "They have a youngster now. A little boy I'll have the pleasure of teaching in another two years. He's likely to be as much of a bruiser as Bertie. Plus, she's pregnant with her second."

"And Trish?"

"She lives in Raleigh with her husband. They met at college a few years ago. She decided to be a teacher, too." Annie smiled brightly. "She's also expecting a baby. Hers is due this Christmas."

"So you really are the last Delacorte," Sam observed.

"Pansy and Trish are still Delacortes," she retorted defensively. "They'll always be Delacortes."

"But their children won't."

"Neither will mine." As though realizing they'd returned to one of the to-be-avoided-at-all-cost topics, she surged to her feet. "This is ridiculous. There must be a way out of here."

"Can't bear to be alone with me?"

He'd said the forbidden, her alarm as transparent as her dress in the sunlight. But still she didn't back down. "No one will know unless you tell. And even then, I doubt anyone would believe it."

He released a bark of laughter. "Still the town virgin, I see. No dirt sticks to our Annie."

Her gaze turned bleak. "It will eventually."

It was the last thing he expected her to say. "Why's that?"

She shrugged, presenting him with a profile as pure and delicate as any he'd ever seen. "It's impossible to stay a saint forever. Eventually, people will realize I'm fallible, just like everyone else."

"And in the meantime, you're bent on giving them advance warning, is that it?"

"Something like that," she confessed.

Now what the hell was behind this? She had a burr stuck in her craw, no question, but he was damned if he knew what had put it there. Myrtle had said Annie'd been acting strangely. Here was the proof. He left the bed and approached. "So you're determined to set the town on its collective ear by riding my motorcycle around town in dresses. What do the good folks of Delacorte Island have to say about that, I wonder?"

"Isn't that precious?" she mimicked. "Keepin' that wicked ol' Beaumont boy's bike up and running."

He flicked a hand at the bright purple stripe that tinted her long blond curls. "And this?"

She swept the strand away from her face. "Look at how it brings out the blue of her eyes."

He tilted his head to one side. "You know...it does."

"Not you, too!" Her pacing took on a frantic quality. "Care to guess what the principal said?"

"Go home and wash the grape punch out of your hair?"

"No. He asked if I wanted to do a hair day at school for all the kids. Can you believe it? They were each supposed to bring in a different flavor of punch so we could color everyone's hair."

"How deflating. So what did you do then?"

From the way she fiddled with the buttons on the front of her dress, he didn't think she'd answer. Finally, she whispered, "A belly ring."

He snorted. "That had to hurt."

"Actually, I passed out when it was half a belly ring, which is why it's now a belly scar."

He tried to look sympathetic but found it impossible to suppress a grin. "I assume the sign in front of Myrtle's was next. How did that read? Something about being the last virgin—"

"Not anymore it doesn't," she hastened to interrupt. "You'll notice the 'v' word has been painted over. Apparently, one doesn't use that word in public. The hens explained that it's vulgar."

"Being vulgar didn't knock you off your pedestal?"

She sighed. "No. I was excused on the grounds that my momma died when I was bitty. For a while, the sign said 'the last unsullied girl in town.' That was thanks to Sheriff Rolly. Then the hens changed it to 'one of the last innocents' presumably because a few of them are under the mistaken impression that their daughters are still—"

"The *v* word?"

Annie shrugged. "It's not my place to disabuse them."

"And why, exactly, did you feel the need to advertise your…ah…unsulliedness? Hoping to attract business?"

"My reputation seems to be of such vital concern to everyone, I thought I'd reassure them on that count, at least." He found her answer an intriguing one. But before he could question her further, she said, "Of course, I wouldn't be in this predicament if I'd given in to you seven years ago."

"I'd be happy to correct the oversight."

"So I've been told. I'll pass, thanks."

"You can try." She might not know it, but she'd sealed her fate with that kiss they'd shared earlier. Any hesitation he might have felt about seducing her had been erased the minute her lips had parted beneath his and she'd welcomed him home. "But you won't succeed."

She eyed him suspiciously. "What do you mean by that?"

He settled onto the bed. "I mean that before I leave town I fully intend to make love to you."

"Quit joking around, Sam. This is hardly the time or place."

"I think it's precisely the time and place. We have everything we need. Privacy, no interruptions for at least a couple of hours, each other and…" He patted the mattress. "A bed."

"You can't be serious!"

Apparently, her desire to end her reign as Saint Annie only went so far. He tilted his head to one side. "Isn't that what you want, what you've been working toward with your antics? You challenge people's conception of you at every turn. All I'm suggesting is that you put your

money where your mouth is. Or in this case, your unsullied self in my bed. I'll take care of the rest.''

"There are limits, Sam."

"But, darlin', I've offered you the perfect solution. If
you want people to treat you differently, just spend the
night in my arms. Then you can take down your sign,
give me back my motorcycle, wash the punch out of your
hair and live a happy life as a fallen woman."

Her chin rose a notch. "No, thank you.'' So polite. So
proper. So typical of a Delacorte. Without another word,
she crossed to the window and stared out.

"Rescue on the horizon?"

"No.'' She squared her shoulders. "Nor do I intend to
wait for someone to rescue me. I can take care of that
myself."

He was off the bed like a shot. "Get away from the
window, Annie."

"Don't fuss, Sam. I used to climb trees all the time."

"You used to *fall* out of trees all the time. That's a
live oak you're thinking about swinging onto. The only
branches within reach wouldn't hold a squirrel."

She leaned out and grabbed at the closest ones.
"They'll hold me."

"No, they won't.'' He didn't bother continuing the
argument. Coming up behind, he wrapped an arm around
her waist just as she threw herself toward a handful of
pencil-thin branches. "Let go, Annie, so I can pull you
in.''

"You let go!"

"If I do, you'll fall."

She glared at him from over her shoulder. "No, if you
do, I'll climb down. Then I can open the door for you."

"I'm not letting go."

She wriggled in his arms, her backside doing serious

damage to his self-control. "This is ridiculous. I can't keep hanging here like this. I'm going to slip."

Enough was enough. "Listen to me, Annie. Let go. Now."

Apparently, she didn't take orders any better than she climbed trees. She flipped her hair from her eyes and clung determinedly to the branches. "Sam Beaumont! This is your last warning. Get your hands off me right this minute or I'm going to kick you where it counts!"

"Shouting is not going to change the situation."

"Maybe not, but it'll make me feel a whole lot—uh-oh."

"Come on, honey. Let go. If I drag you inside, you're going to end up with a palm full of splinters."

"Er...Sam?"

"You don't want splinters on top of everything else, now do you?"

"Sam, maybe you better let go."

"Not a—"

"*Sam!*"

He heard it then—outraged shouts, followed by the distinctive crash of a front door being ripped open and slammed against the side of the house. Undoubtedly, their visitors had seen Annie hanging out the window, seen him trying to pull her in, heard her shouts and put a dangerously wrong construction on what was happening—dangerously wrong for him, that was. An instant later, feet pounded on the stairs. It sounded like a stampede. Actually, it sounded more like a posse. He'd gotten familiar with that particular type of commotion. Something about Annie must bring out a lynch-mob mentality in folk.

Annie cleared her throat. "I think you can go ahead and pull me in now."

"I gather we're about to be rescued?"

"Well, one of us, at any rate." She peeked up at him. "And they didn't look happy about it, either."

Seconds later, Sheriff Rolly pounded on the bedroom door. "Open up right this minute."

Sam swung Annie back into the bedroom. "I'm afraid that's easier said than done, Sheriff."

There was a momentary scuffle and then Ben could be heard asking, "Where's the knob? What's he done to the door?"

"I'm only going to warn you one more time, Beaumont. Either you open up right now and turn that poor girl loose or I'll arrest you for...for..."

"Kissing Annie?" Sam offered helpfully.

"Oh, great," she muttered. "You just had to go and say that, didn't you?"

"It's the truth, isn't it?"

"You didn't kiss me here. You kissed me at Myrtle's."

"Oh, right. Remind me to rectify the situation. I wouldn't want to be accused of lying as well as sullying."

"I haven't been sullied!"

"Did you hear that?" Rolly shouted. "She's been sullied! Stand back, boys. I'm gonna shoot the lousy SOB."

CHAPTER THREE

ANNIE gaped at the door. "Did he say...? Sheriff Rawling! You don't seriously intend to shoot—"

Apparently, Sam thought the sheriff meant just that. Hooking an arm around her waist, he swept her clear of the doorway. "Let's not do anything foolish, Sheriff."

"Foolish, is it? As far as I'm concerned, shootin' you is the smartest thing I'm ever liable to do. Ain't that right, boys?"

"Now, Rolly," Ben could be heard to placate, "you just can't start blasting away at folks."

"Might hit our Annie," came a rather belabored third voice.

"Listen to the mayor, Sheriff," Sam inserted. "Somebody could get hurt."

Rolly chuckled. "That's what I'm countin' on, son."

Annie attempted to fight free of Sam's hold. The minute she succeeded, he swept her back into his arms, keeping her well clear of the door. Realizing it was pointless to continue struggling, she called out. "Mayor Pike? Is that you?"

The breathless voice spoke up again. "You betcha, Annie. Whoo-ee, but it's a hot one today. Thought all those stairs were going to do me in for sure."

Annie released a long-suffering sigh. "Would someone please open the door? The knob fell out and we're stuck in here."

"How'd the Beaumont boy manage that?" the sheriff demanded.

"He didn't do a thing. *I* did it. Or rather the wind did. It blew the door closed and trapped us. Now would you mind helping me *undo* it?"

There was a whispered discussion on the other side. "Miss Annie?"

"Yes, Ben?"

"If you'll push the knob in from your end, we'll see if we can't put the one out here in from this end. If that doesn't work, though, I'll have to get some tools out of my truck." He cleared his throat. "It...ah...might take a while."

"Take all the time you need," Sam insisted. "We can keep ourselves busy, no problem."

"I'm *fine*, Ben," Annie hastened to say. "We're both fine."

Sam winked at her. "Just enjoying each other's company."

"Would you stop that?" she ordered in a furious undertone. "You're giving them the wrong idea and they're upset enough. If I didn't know better, I'd think you wanted them to..." Her eyes narrowed.

"Believe I was busy ruining you?" He tucked her up in his arms good and proper. "We have the perfect opportunity. We even have witnesses. What do you say? Shall we get down to business?"

"Miss Annie? Are you still there?"

Barely. "Yes, Ben. I'm here."

"Have you found the knob?"

"I'm still looking for it." She lowered her voice. "Let go, Sam. You've had your fun. Now let's leave before things get serious."

His expression turned wry. "Too late. They got serious a long time ago. Besides, I still have that small oversight to correct, remember? You wouldn't want me to be accused of lying on top of everything else, would you?''

"What oversight is that?'' she asked. As if she didn't know! Telling the three men they'd been in here kissing was the spark that had set the sheriff's temper on fire in the first place.

"This one...."

He urged her closer, eliminating the few scant inches separating them. Lowering his head, he sealed her mouth with his. She really should protest. But somehow she couldn't quite gather the wherewithal. Why did he keep doing this? And why did she keep responding like a woman desperate for his taste? Perhaps because she was. Perhaps because seven years had starved her, left her with a hankering so deep and so powerful that it would take a lifetime to satisfy.

His hands slipped into her hair, lifting the weight away from the nape of her neck. He wound the curls between his fingers, anchoring her firmly against him. Not that she was going anywhere. Everything she'd ever wanted or ever could want she'd find there in his arms, with his lips consuming hers.

With a rumble of pleasure, his mouth slipped from hers to follow the line of her jaw. Her groan stirred the air between them. "Just give me a second,'' she pleaded. "Just one more—oh, yes, Sam, right there—second and then I'll make you stop.''

His hands crept upward, drifting dangerously close to her breasts. "Take all the time you need, sweetheart. I'm in no hurry. But whatever you do, stop me quietly or prepare to dodge flying lead.''

Her lashes fluttered downward and she shifted ever so slightly to the left, just enough so his hand would collide with its goal. "Lead?''

"Bullet lead. I don't trust our sheriff to behave himself with a loaded weapon." He busied himself feathering kisses along her neckline. "Now that I think about it, I'm beginning to suspect good ol' Rolly's a few bullets short of a full clip."

Annie's lips parted to reply, but somehow the words got lost in her sigh of pleasure. She fought to regain her sanity—an easy enough task. Or it would have been if Sam hadn't scattered the bits and pieces of her reason to the four winds. Or if he hadn't skated his mouth in the general direction of where his hands were working their wicked magic. The scrape of his teeth elicited a muffled shriek. *There, there, right damned there*! begged the part of her intent on destruction. But some truly rotten part of her—the part determined to retain her saintly halo, no doubt—protested. "Don't," she choked out.

Sam's black Beaumont eyes beckoned her toward the sweetest of dooms. "Don't stop?" he asked hopefully.

"Don't stop. No. Yes."

He grinned. "Got it. Always happy to oblige a lady."

Rolly hammered on the door. At least she assumed it was Sheriff Rawling. None of the others had hands large enough to cause such a commotion. "Annie Delacorte? What the hell's going on in there, girl?"

Her ruination, she was tempted to say. But to admit as much would only bring out guns and bullets and cause more harm than she could bear. "No more, Sam." *Please, no more*! "Our company's getting impatient."

"Tough. They weren't invited to this particular party, so they can stay where they are until we're done."

She tried to muffle her laugh, with only limited success. "I'm serious, Sam. You have to stop now." She eased back, feeling the painful tug of her hair still tight within his grasp.

The swift intake of her breath must have alerted him. With a touch so gentle it threatened to bring tears to her eyes, Sam untangled his fingers from her curls. Bending, he picked up the knob from the floor and silently handed it over.

"I found it," she announced, praying the door would muffle the emotions rippling through her voice.

"That a girl, Annie. Come on over to the door and slip it into the hole."

"She's not going anywhere, Sheriff. Not until you lose that gun."

"Now, Sam. I'm not planning to shoot Annie." There was a significant pause before he added cheerfully, "Just you."

Annie folded her arms across her chest and glared at the door—a decidedly futile gesture since they couldn't witness her annoyance. "In that case, I'm not coming out," she announced in a voice her kindergartners would recognize. It was the "behave or else" tone that never failed to have them scrambling for their seats.

"Aw, Annie. I was just funnin' with the boy."

"I want your promise, Sheriff Rawling, that you're not going to lay a single finger on Sam. No fists, no arrests, no guns, and especially no bullets."

He heaved a sigh that could only be read as disappointment. "Fine, fine. I promise. I'm taking off my gun belt. Hear? You can look through the hole and see I've set it on the floor."

Kneeling, she checked to confirm she wouldn't have to do something foolishly noble, like fling herself in front of a bullet intended for Sam. Reassured the sheriff had done as he said, she slipped the knob into the hole, holding it steady. "Okay, my end's in." A moment later, she felt the knob jiggle and slowly turn.

"Stand clear," the mayor warned.

An instant later, a shoulder impacted the door and it flew open. The sheriff was the first to tumble into the room. Ben and the mayor followed close behind.

"Annie! Are you all right?" Ben asked anxiously.

She reassured him with a smile. "I'm just fine, thanks. Shall we go?"

Mayor Pike ambled over to the bed and stared down at it with a frown. Then he eyed Annie with equal care—particularly her dress, which she suspected was in as serious disarray as the bed. Oops. Glancing at his companions, Pike jerked his head toward the rumpled bedcovers before addressing Annie. "You run along now, my dear. We want to talk to Beaumont in private."

"This isn't the best place to conduct a conversation," Sam observed mildly.

Just great. Four pit bulls all kenneled in one room. What were the odds of everyone getting out in one piece? "Since I came with Sam, I'm afraid I'll have to wait until he's ready to leave." She crossed to the rickety chair. Holding her breath and offering up a quick prayer, she carefully sat. It held, allowing her to maintain her regal posture instead of flailing around on the floor. "Anything you have to discuss with Sam, you can say in front of me."

"Gentlemen?" Sam spoke up once more. "I strongly recommend we take this discussion outside."

"So you'll have the chance to jump on that bike of yours and take off?" Rolly argued. "That's not gonna happen, son."

"No. I was more concerned about—"

An earsplitting bang sounded behind them, followed by a familiar clang as a pair of knobs hit the floor.

"—the door slamming closed again."

Annie uttered a most unladylike word, not caring in the least that she was the focus of three scandalized gazes plus Sam's highly amused one. "That tears it," she said to no one in particular.

"Now, Miss Annie," Ben attempted to placate, "let's not get your druthers in an uproar."

"Too late. My druthers are already in an uproar." Of course, some of that might be due to Sam-of-the-magical-fingers, but the town's leading citizens didn't really need to know that. "How do you intend to get us out of this mess?" she demanded.

"Well, now. I'm sure someone will venture by before too long," the sheriff offered. "Eventually, Bertie will figure out I've gone missing."

Sam made himself comfortable on the bed again. "Why don't you radio him?"

The sheriff reached for his belt, then realized where he'd left it. He cursed roundly before breaking off and shooting Annie a sheepish glance. "Beg your pardon, Miss Annie."

"I think she's heard the words before," Sam offered, folding his arms behind his head. "Hell, I believe she's even said a few. Right here in this very room, if I'm not mistaken."

Perhaps a good scolding was in order. With luck, it would deflect attention from her small lapse in manners. "If you three had listened to Sam instead of bursting in here like the Three Musketeers—" For some reason, that elicited a blush from the men in question. "—we wouldn't be in this predicament."

"Yes, ma'am," Ben agreed. "It's just Sam there…and the bed…" His blush deepened. "And your dress."

She gave the four men her iciest look. "I see. Well, there's a perfectly good explanation for all that." Seeing their fascinated expressions, she decided this might be a good time to execute a graceful exit. "Not that any of you deserve an explanation. Instead, I'll do what you four have failed to do and get us out of here."

Sam sat up abruptly. "Annie—"

"And this time *no one* better stop me."

Sam was off the bed in a flash. But he was too late. Hoping her poor, underused muscles could still execute the ballet lessons she'd endured a full score of years earlier, Annie leaped with all the elegance of a hamstrung gazelle straight out the window.

"I don't know what you were thinking," Aunt Myrtle fussed, dabbing antiseptic with a liberal hand. "You could have broken something."

Annie grimaced. "It's just a few scratches." Or maybe a few dozen. All of which were profusely leaking icky red stuff. Not that she bothered to examine them too closely. Giving her injuries that much attention might cause her to do something silly. Like faint. Who would have thought all those bitty twigs could do so much damage? Well, other than Sam, that was.

"You should have guessed that oak wouldn't support your weight," Myrtle said, resuming her chiding.

"I did warn her," Sam offered.

"I'm sure you did. You always were a good boy."

He all but smirked. "Yes, ma'am."

Annie gave her annoyance free rein, hoping it would provide a distraction from her various cuts and bruises. "Going out the window was the only way to rescue everyone from the bedroom. If I hadn't climbed down the tree—"

"Fallen out of the tree," Sam corrected.

"*Gotten down*. The rest of you would still be battling it out in the bedroom."

"What were you doing in Sam's bedroom in the first place?" Myrtle asked, shifting her attention from Annie's arm to her bruised knee. More of the reddish-orange medicine polka-dotted her skin. She just ought to bathe in the stuff. It would be simpler.

Sam nodded sagely. "Ah...the million-dollar question. She was up to no good, I'll bet."

"You should know!" Annie retorted indignantly. "You were there, too."

"Exactly. Up to no good."

"Don't listen to him, Aunt Myrtle." She tried hard not to wince, refusing to give Sam the satisfaction. "I was showing him all the damage to Soundings when the door blew shut and the knob fell out."

"That's our story, Myrtle, and we're sticking to it." Sam gave Annie a teasing wink. "Right, sweetheart?"

"Oh, stop it. People might think you're serious."

"People won't think I'm serious. They'll know I am." He tilted his head to one side. "Odd, isn't it? I'll bet this will be the first time anyone's ever doubted your word. They'll all suspect you're covering up what really happened in that bedroom for fear of destroying your unblemished reputation. Maybe we should take down your sign. That would *really* give them something to talk about."

If she could have reached him, she'd have boxed his ears. "What happened is...nothing happened," she explained for Myrtle's benefit.

Sam shook his head. "Shame on you, Miss Annie. You know full well that's not the complete truth. Aren't you skipping a detail or two?"

Of course she was skipping a detail or two! "No, I'm

not," she lied without compunction. "Right after the door slammed closed, Ben and Sheriff Rolly and Mayor Pike came riding up the drive to my rescue as if they were the Three Musketeers or something." Sam and Aunt Myrtle began to laugh and she looked from one to the other in bewilderment. "What? What did I say?"

"It's your reference to them as the Three Musketeers," Myrtle explained. "That's what the boys call themselves."

It was strange to hear the town's leading citizens described as "boys". Funnier still to hear they called themselves Musketeers. "You're kidding, right?"

Myrtle struggled to keep a straight face, finally giving it up as a lost cause. "They don't realize anyone knows, but of course everyone does. We just pretend not to so we don't embarrass the poor boys." She gave a genteel snort. "But I mean, really. What are we supposed to think when they run around shouting 'One for all and all for one'?"

Annie stared, fascinated. "They do? Are you serious?"

"Well," Myrtle admitted with a mischievous grin, "perhaps they don't shout it. It's just whenever they come up with some harebrained scheme, that's what they'll say to signify agreement. Then off they go, stirring up a fine mess, all in the name of honor or some such."

Annie frowned. "Now you've made me curious. What do you suppose they were doing at Soundings?"

"Isn't it obvious?" Sam asked. "Rescuing you."

"Yes, but...how did they know we were in trouble?"

Myrtle chuckled. "They're Musketeers. No doubt they have special senses that alert them when trouble is at hand."

Sam's good humor faded. "They don't need to go

looking for trouble. It'll find them soon enough. In fact, I'll see to it personally."

"Don't start that again," Annie said. "They were trying to help."

"No, they were trying to shoot me."

"Only Sheriff Rawling. Ben Drake and Mayor Pike were being very understanding."

"So understanding they got us trapped in the room again. If the mayor hadn't been intent on giving me a dressing-down and Rolly determined to start a brawl, the door wouldn't have blown shut a second time and put us back in our initial predicament."

"Men can be very silly," Myrtle observed. "But at least everyone is all right."

"Only because I rescued them," Annie muttered. "If I'd been smart, I'd have left them there a spell and come back in a few days to clean up the pieces that remained."

"It would have spared you some gossip," Sam agreed.

Annie looked up in alarm. "What gossip?"

"You haven't heard?"

"I haven't been to Drake's Supermarket since we left Soundings." This couldn't be good. Not coming on the heels of the last bit of gossip making the rounds. "What are they saying?"

"Everyone's talking about how you threw yourself out the window to save yourself from a fate worse than death." He shook his head in disgust. "Saint Annie's legend lives on."

"Oh, shut up."

"Shut up? You can do worse than that. I know you can." He grinned. "And so do Rolly, Ben and Mayor Pike."

"Somehow I doubt they're going to tell on me," Annie said morosely.

"True enough. Even if they did, I doubt anyone would believe them. Not now."

"This is ridiculous." She winced as Myrtle dug out another splinter. "How did you survive it all those years?" she asked the older woman.

"How did I survive what?"

"Sainthood."

"Ah, but I was just Aunt Myrtle. Never a saint."

"But you could do no wrong, either. Didn't that worry you? Didn't you ever wonder what would happen once people realized you were just human?" Once the town had discovered how "human" Sam's mother had been, she'd been ostracized, a fact that had had a profound effect on her son, especially since he'd paid the ultimate price for his mother's "sins."

"I am just human and everyone does know it."

"But you're so good. So kind. What if people woke up one day and decided you weren't good and kind anymore?"

Myrtle's dark eyes glittered with laughter. "Silly girl. It wouldn't change who I am. It would only change what others thought of me. Haven't you figured that out yet?"

"What's this all about, Annie?" Sam asked abruptly.

"Nothing," she said with a shrug. "Tired of being Saint Annie, I guess."

"I keep telling you. Next time, don't throw yourself out the window to escape my evil clutches. Maybe then you'll be that wicked Delacorte girl. Would you like that better?"

Yes! "I just don't want to disappoint people." Which they would be when they found out the truth. But she couldn't very well tell Sam that. Although chances were he'd discover it on his own soon enough.

*   *   *

Sam slipped into Myrtle's house, taking extra care to keep his passage through the darkened rooms as silent as possible. It was well past midnight and he knew the two women would have turned in hours ago. He'd have, too, if it hadn't been for a small business matter he'd needed to rectify. He'd been surprised as hell when the Musketeers had shown up at his place to "rescue" Annie. It seemed they hadn't been as intimidated by his threats as he'd assumed. His mouth tilted to one side. He hadn't counted on the fact that they were three decent, well-meaning men who felt genuine love and concern for the town "saint".

Not that he could blame them. He had pretty strong feelings for her, as well.

But it still left an intriguing puzzle, one he intended to solve. When he'd asked them how they'd known he and Annie were alone at Soundings, they'd become annoyingly closedmouthed. Apparently, their code of honor required that they protect their source as well as Annie. Not that it mattered. He'd have plenty of opportunities to accomplish his goal in the next several weeks. Just as he'd have plenty of time to settle old scores.

Soundlessly, he crept upstairs, doing his level best not to disturb Annie and Myrtle. His old bedroom was at the end of the hall, the windows facing the woods. His former bride-to-be wasn't the only one who made a habit of escaping from bedrooms via a conveniently placed tree. In his misbegotten youth, he'd sneaked out of this one on a regular basis. Of course, he'd managed to climb down the tree, rather than tumble from it. Easing open his bedroom door, he slipped inside, not bothering with the light.

Yanking off his shirt, he tossed it aside. His jeans soon followed and he left them where they dropped. The bed

beckoned and he stretched, exhaustion hounding his
every step. Moonlight guided him and he sank onto the
mattress. Heaven help him, it felt good to be home.
Because despite everything, Delacorte Island had always
been his home. It had a uniqueness he hadn't found anywhere else. Even the air was unique, scented with ocean
and marsh and tropical humidity.

Falling back onto the pillow, he folded his arms behind
his head, facing a disconcerting truth that had dogged him
unceasingly for the past year. He was tired of Wall Street.
Tired of the frantic pace, clipped accents and endless
workdays. He hadn't realized how much he longed to
hear the slow drawls that flavored the South, to simply
set a spell and watch the local kids play a game of base-
ball. To stroll on the beach at sunset and catch a wave
or two. To gather a soft, willing woman in his arms and
thoroughly ruin her. And then, maybe, to do it all over
again.

He'd missed Delacorte Island. Missed it more than he
thought possible. And in that moment, a bone-deep cer-
tainty took hold. He wasn't going to leave. Nor would
he be thrown off. This was his home and he intended to
stay put. In the morning, he'd contact his partner, Diana
Starr, and confirm his intention to sell his share of the
business. She wasn't going to be happy, but that couldn't
be helped. Diana was a savvy New Yorker. She'd find
someone to replace him soon enough. No doubt they'd
be beating down her door, since she was every bit as
good at making money as was he.

His decision made, Sam rolled over, only then realizing he was a breath away from accomplishing the last
item on his list—to ruin a willing woman. Curled up in
a ball at his side, indulging in the deep sleep of the innocent, was Annie.

For a full sixty seconds, he considered taking the noble path and finding which room Myrtle had prepared for him. But he swiftly gave it up. Hell, he'd been born the son of a bastard and had worked hard to earn a reputation to match his birthright. Why should he change now? Besides…he'd promised Annie, promised he'd do his level best to compromise her. And after all, he *was* a man of his word.

With infinite care, he drew her into his arms. And while hers would surely be the sleep of the innocent, he didn't doubt his would be the sleep of the damned.

Not that he cared. Spooning a lushly curved backside tight against his belly and thighs, he decided it was one hell of a way to go. Yes sirree. One hell of a sweet way.

Annie was slow to wake, which was unusual enough. But something else felt odd, something she couldn't quite put her finger on. For one thing, it was later than it should have been, the sun filling the room with a brightness that warned she'd slept well past seven. Maybe that was it. It was also warm. Almost hot. And yet the windows were wide open and a light breeze stirred the curtains. Or perhaps it was how the covers had tangled around her, binding her waist and legs. With a growl of annoyance, she kicked out at them.

"Hey, watch it, will you?" Sam muttered. "You could hurt someone doing that." Instantly, she began flailing. Not that it got her anywhere. He rolled over, wrapping his arms around her. "Let me guess. You're not a morning person, are you?"

It took her thirty full seconds to find her voice and couple it with a brain that seemed to be badly misfiring. "You're in my bed! What are you doing here?"

"It's my bed."

"It used to be your bed. Now it's mine, and I want you out of it!''

"You know...you have a real annoying habit of taking what belongs to me." He rubbed the shadow of dark whiskers clinging to his jaw. "We're definitely gonna have to talk about that."

"Get out of my bed!" she shrieked.

"Keep yelling like that and you'll have the whole town in here. Then your reputation will be in shreds." He lifted an eyebrow. "Or is that what you want?"

Clapping a hand over her mouth, she glared, momentarily stymied.

"What's that you said?" he teased. "I couldn't quite catch it."

"I said you're a pain in the neck, Sam Beaumont," she complained around her fingers. "Everything was fine around here until you decided to come back."

"First, I don't think you said 'neck'. I do believe you were swearing again, Annie Delacorte." Before she could deny it, he continued, "And second, things aren't fine around here."

She regarded him warily. "What do you mean?"

"Did you really think Myrtle wouldn't tell me?"

Uh-oh. "Tell you what?"

"About how oddly you've been acting."

Annie couldn't contain her shock. "She actually got in touch with you about me?"

"I believe her exact words were, 'Annie's got more tribulations than Horse Swallow Swamp has skeeters.'"

"I guarantee there are more mosquitoes in Horse Swallow Swamp. Heck, there are more swallowed-up horses in that swamp than problems in my life."

"Now why don't I believe you?"

She fiddled with the edge of the sheet. "You were

never a particularly trusting soul, Sam. Now that I think about it, it's probably one of your greatest failings.''

"I'm devastated." He brushed a tangle of curls from her face. "Come on, Annie. Myrtle wouldn't have asked me to come back without cause. Now tell me what's wrong."

"You…" She moistened her lips, looking everywhere but into Sam's black eyes. If she did, she'd be lost. "You came back because of me?"

"Yup."

"Because you thought something was wrong?"

"Among other things."

That intrigued her. "What other things?"

He shook his head. "Not so fast, sweetheart. You answer my questions first. What's wrong? Why have you been acting so strangely? You realize you have Myrtle worried sick, don't you?"

"I didn't mean to. Really, Sam. There's nothing wrong." At least nothing she could discuss with him. Or anyone else, for that matter.

"So it's all Myrtle's imagination?"

She couldn't agree with that. It wouldn't be fair to the woman she'd come to love more than any other person on the island. "I wouldn't say that, exactly."

"Nor would I. Not when I come back to find you speeding around town like a reckless teenager and coloring your hair every shade in the rainbow and piercing your belly button. What's up?"

"Nothing!"

She had to escape. Right now, before he found a way to coax the truth from her. Shoving at his arms, she attempted to wiggle free of his embrace. And that's when she realized something quite deliciously shocking.

Sam was as naked as the day he was born.

Annie couldn't remember when she'd moved so fast. One minute she was snuggled cozily in Sam's arms. The next she was halfway across the room, as jittery as a scalded cat.

CHAPTER FOUR

"CLOTHES. Clothes. Clothes." Annie waved frantically at the pertinent parts of his anatomy. When that didn't achieve much in the way of action, she clapped her hands over her eyes. "For the sake of my sanity, you need to put on some clothes, Sam." Actually, he didn't. But she didn't dare confess as much, considering where such an admission would undoubtedly lead. Like back to bed.

"Sure. As soon as you answer my question."

Question? *What* question? Right now, she didn't remember her own name, let alone anything he might have asked. "Fine. Yes."

"Yes?"

"Whatever you asked. The answer's yes."

He sighed, and she heard the squeak of the bedsprings as he left the bed. "You haven't a clue what I asked, do you?"

"No. Now will you put on your clothes?"

"They're on." The minute she'd peeled her hands away from her eyes, he added, "Sort of."

"Sort of" meant he'd yanked on his jeans, but they still gaped in a most provocative manner. "That's not fair," she informed him, struggling to pull her attention from the line of hair running riot down the flat planes of his stomach.

"Life's tough. Get used to it." He waited until she'd dragged her gaze into more appropriate territory before continuing. "Just to refresh your memory, I believe I asked you what's wrong."

66

"You mean aside from waking up and finding a naked man in my bed?"

He grinned. "Not a daily occurrence?"

"No, as you darned well know."

He snapped his fingers. "Right. The sign professing your vir—"

"—tue!"

"Gesundheit."

"Virtue," she repeated. "And nothing's wrong. I'm perfectly happy with my life." For some reason, she found it hard to be nonchalant when a half-naked man filled her bedroom with his presence. Or maybe it was her skimpy nightie. Realizing she was providing Sam with as interesting a view as he was providing her, she snatched up a robe and shoved her arms into the sleeves. "I share a home with the sweetest woman in the world. I have a job I adore. I live on one of the prettiest islands in the country. What could possibly be wrong?"

"What about marriage and children?"

She couldn't believe he had the nerve to ask. But then, Sam Beaumont had nerve to spare. He always had. She'd never known anyone or anything that could intimidate him. "I'll pass, thanks."

His eyes narrowed. "You don't plan to marry? To have children?"

"No." She sounded so cold and final, but that couldn't be helped. It was how she felt.

His concern was unmistakable. "Now I know something's wrong. You adore children. You used to say you'd like a dozen."

She made a passing stab at levity. "I was eighteen years old and clearly insane. Anyone who hopes for a dozen children would have to be." She shrugged. "Instead, I teach several dozen. That's quite sufficient, thanks.''

He approached. "You don't want to marry? To ripen with your husband's child?"

To ripen... It was such a provocative description. "No." She cleared her throat and tried again. "No, I don't want that."

"You don't want to feel your baby move within you, either?" He stopped mere inches away, the heat of his body stealing over her, dissipating the inner chill. "To feel each kick, to nurture it close inside you, tucked beneath your heart?"

Why did he keep asking? She'd answered already. Didn't he know how his questions were ripping her apart? How much they hurt? He stood too close to escape, his scrutiny too intense to avoid. "Stop it, Sam," she ordered in a low tone.

"Don't you want to bear a son and daughter someday and cradle them in your arms? To take them to your breast and nurse them?"

"No, no, no! Children aren't necessary to make one's life complete." How many times had she told herself that? And how many times had she secretly railed against that fate?

"Then why are you crying?" He reached out and captured a tear from the tip of her lashes, a tear she hadn't even realized she'd shed. "Are you infertile? Is that why you changed your mind, why you sent me away?"

She stumbled back a step, bumping into an oak dresser. "How can you ask a question like that?"

"Is that what happened?" His voice had sharpened, demanding an answer.

"As far as I know, I'm perfectly capable of having

children.'' She fought for composure. ''I keep telling
you. Everything's fine.''

''No, it's not. And I suspect it hasn't been for a very
long time.'' His arms slipped around her, corralling her
within a circle of warmth and security. ''Something happened seven years ago and whatever it was caused you
to send me away.''

''You're right. Something did happen.'' She forced out
the lie. ''I changed my mind.''

''Don't, Annie,'' he said quietly, forcefully. ''Whatever it is…it's still there. And it's keeping you from
me.''

She saw it then. Saw the pain lurking in the darkness
of his eyes, the rawness behind the devil-may-care grin.
She'd done that to him. She'd hurt him with her actions
seven years ago. Any other man would have hated her
as a result, or written her off as trouble to be avoided.
Instead, Sam had kept a wary distance. Yet the minute
Myrtle had called, he'd climbed on his bike and ridden
hell-bent for leather for Delacorte Island. Back to her. It
hurt. Oh, how it hurt.

''Let it go, Sam. Tell Myrtle I'm just being as wild as
a Dela…'' Her voice cracked, her words caught in an
unexpected storm of emotion.

He held her close, cradling her against his shoulder.
''Sweetheart, don't,'' he murmured. ''It's okay. We'll
work it out together.''

She pushed his hands away. ''You listen to me, Sam
Beaumont.'' She fought for the last shreds of control, the
words escaping in a torrent. ''I'm being as wild as a
Delacorte can be. That might not be much by Beaumont
standards, but I assure you, I'm not the saint most people
think.''

His smile was so tender it wounded. "You're a wild one all right."

Her laughter had a desperate edge. "But that's not saying a lot, is it?" Why, oh why, couldn't she succeed at something as simple as being outrageous? "I might ride a motorcycle, but I can't even do it without a helmet or without making sure my dress won't blow up over my head."

"I hate to tell you this," he admitted, fighting off a smile, "but that minor detail pleases me no end."

"And my hair!"

"What about your hair?"

"Did I dye all of it? I thought about it. I wanted to. But did I?" She grabbed a hank and waved it at him. "No! In the end I only had the nerve for this silly little stripe."

"But it's a cute silly little stripe."

"Stop it! You don't understand. I put up a sign, then I let everyone paint over it. I got a belly ring. Or tried to." Her breath came in a deep, shuddering gasp. "I couldn't even manage that."

"So you have a belly scar. That's pretty daring."

"Not for a Beaumont. A Beaumont would have gotten the whole dang—damn ring. I just can't get it right, can I? I can't even swear right." Ducking beneath the circle of his arms, she raced for the door.

"Annie, wait!"

But she didn't wait. She didn't dare. She'd said far too much as it was. Heaven help her, what was she going to do? How was she going to handle Sam's nonstop probing? To her relief, he didn't immediately follow. She could only hope he was fastening his pants and throwing on a shirt. She'd never realized how disconcerting naked skin could be—at least Sam's naked skin.

Gaining the kitchen, she made a beeline for the coffeemaker on the counter. Just what she needed. Myrtle must have brewed some before going off to the community center for her morning of volunteer work, bless her heart. With shaking hands, Annie poured a mug and added several heaping spoonfuls of sugar. Normally, she'd have taken it with milk. But right now, strong, sweet and black seemed the better choice. It hit her stomach like battery acid.

"Mind if I join you?" Sam asked from the doorway, regarding her the way one might a hissing kitten. Cautious, but not terribly intimidated.

"Of course not." So polite, so courteous. If she didn't know better, she'd have sworn her manners had been bred in her genes. She poured a second cup of coffee and handed it to Sam. To her relief, her hands hardly trembled at all. "I assume you still drink it unvarnished?"

He leaned a hip against the counter in a casual manner, but Annie noticed he looked far from relaxed. "Now there's an expression I haven't heard in a while. Makes me downright homesick."

"Do you miss it?"

"Living here?" At her nod, he inclined his head. "Yeah, I do. I was thinking about that last night."

"When you invaded my bed?" Oops. Maybe she shouldn't have brought that up.

"My bed."

Her temper flared again. It did that a lot lately. "Oh, please. Don't hand me any of that nonsense about wandering into the wrong bedroom."

"I wasn't—"

"That old trick ranks right up there with running out of gas and getting a flat tire."

"In case you've forgotten, I didn't wander into your

bed by mistake. I did it on purpose. That room was mine, if you recall.''

"'Was' being the operative word.''

He eyed her over the rim of his gently steaming mug, his gaze uncomfortably intent. ''Interesting that neither you nor Myrtle bothered to tell me about the change.'' He lifted an eyebrow. ''Or was this another one of your attempts to prove how wild you are? Did you hope to get that sign changed?''

"Trust me, Sam Beaumont. You won't have anything to do with the removal of my sign!''

"You're kidding yourself on that score, Miss Delacorte. I intend to take care of your precious sign personally.''

"Not a chance. You're the last man I'm likely to invite into my bed.''

"Too late, remember? You should thank your lucky stars that no one knows we shared pajamas last night. Otherwise your reputation would be history.'' He slid his mug across the counter toward her. ''And in case there's any doubt in your mind, you'd have loved every minute.''

"Oh!'' She dumped more coffee into his mug, splashing as much onto the counter as into his cup. ''We did *not* share pajamas as you so eloquently put it.''

His Beaumont grin was back in place. ''True enough, since at least one of us was buck naked.''

"If you dare tell anyone—''

"Have we arrived at an inopportune moment?'' an amused voice asked from the doorway.

Annie jerked around, hot color washing into her cheeks. ''Pansy! How long have you been there?''

"Bertie and I just arrived.'' She gave her husband a swift elbow. ''Didn't we, sweetie?''

"Sure did," he lied gallantly, ducking to fit his six-foot-five-inch frame beneath the doorway. "Hey, Annie. Beaumont."

Sam inclined his head. "Hinkle. Belated congratulations on your marriage. And I understand your family's expanding?"

Pansy patted her swollen stomach in satisfaction. "Number two's due any time now. And before I forget, I expect you to stop by and meet number one, Sam, just as soon as you're situated. Right now, the bruiser's busy driving Grandma Rosie insane, so you can be grateful I'm sparing you his antics."

"Momma doesn't mind," Bertie protested. "She's crazy about the little fella."

Pansy chuckled. "Little? That kid would do a first-grader proud. Unfortunately, he's got a temper to match his size." She slanted her husband a teasing glance. "Comes by it naturally is my guess."

Bertie turned a dull red. "That was a long time ago. I haven't lost my temper in ages."

"True enough. It must be...oh, a whole week since you cussed out that poor, innocent lawn mower." Pansy turned her twinkling gaze on Annie. "Interesting getup. Something you want to tell us about?"

Oh, shoot. "I...I was just getting a cup of coffee before I dressed."

Pansy winked. "Got it. Well, we won't tattle. Right, Bertie?"

Bertie didn't look nearly as tattleproof. But another elbow to the ribs brought him around. "Sure thing, honey."

Annie resorted to schoolteacher mode. Lifting her chin, she shot her relatives her most intimidating look, which proved something of a challenge when dressed in a skimpy nightie and robe. "I'm afraid I wasn't expecting company. If you'll excuse me, I'll go change."

"You forget," Pansy pointed out, "we're not company. Family's allowed to drop by uninvited and poke their noses where they don't belong any time they get the notion." She waved Annie off and crossed to the refrigerator. "I don't suppose Myrtle's been doing any baking?"

Her question didn't require an answer. Pansy could root out every sweet in the house without any help from big sister. Pregnancy had given her an extra sense in that regard. Hastening to her bedroom, Annie closed the door and swiftly stripped. Normally, she'd have hopped in the shower, but this morning she didn't dare. Heaven only knew what trouble would brew downstairs in the few extra minutes it would take to duck under the spray. Just taking the time to pluck a dress from the closet and toss it over her head would give Pansy plenty enough opportunity to run her mouth.

"...Pops was sure you were going to work your way right through all three Delacorte girls," Pansy was busily telling Sam as Annie tripped down the stairs to the kitchen. Apparently, pregnancy had done far more than play havoc with her sister's taste buds. It had also completely eradicated all sense of propriety. There was no other explanation. "I can't imagine why he thought that when he knew how I felt about Bertie."

"Pansy! I'm sure Pops thought no such thing." Annie glanced at Sam in concern. Propriety be hanged and clothes be damned. She never should have left him alone with Pansy.

He didn't show any expression other than a faint amusement. But she knew him well enough to see the signs he usually managed to keep hidden from others—

signs that warned he wasn't taking Pansy's comments nearly as equably as he let on. Sister dear had clearly hit a nerve. Sam held his coffee mug in a white-knuckled grip and his eyes, though half-concealed by his lashes, were stormy. Even his posture spoke of someone on the edge of explosive action. Annie silently groaned.

Sam's relationship with her father had been hostile in the extreme. Delacortes didn't associate with Beaumonts, Pops had explained on more than one occasion. But worse, Sam's mother had been illegitimate, and the blemish to his birthright had been thrown in his face with annoying regularity, usually resulting in a fierce brawl—a brawl Sam invariably won. In fact, it had been one of the main reasons he'd never allowed his desire for her to get out of hand. He'd told her repeatedly that he'd never father a bastard child and the only way to make sure of it was through abstinence. When she became pregnant with his baby, they'd be legally wed. The knowledge of all she'd lost haunted her to this day, for they'd never marry and she'd never bear his children. She couldn't.

Shooting Pansy a quelling glance, Annie crossed to Sam's side and peeled the mug from his hand. "Let me freshen that for you," she murmured, skating a hand around his waist and rubbing his back reassuringly. Her position blocked her actions from the others—not that she cared if they saw. She was too angry to care. For Sam's sake, though, she didn't want anyone to realize how deeply Pansy's words had wounded.

Imperceptibly, he relaxed. "Thanks, I'd appreciate that."

Annie shot a quick look toward Bertie to see if he'd picked up on Sam's grating tone. Apparently, he had. For such a big lug, he could be amazingly sensitive when he chose. "Let's go, Pansy."

His wife blinked in surprise. "Why? We just got here."

"You've inflicted yourself on Annie and Sam long enough." He held out his hand. "Beaumont. Glad to have you back on the island."

"Thanks, Bertie." Sam took the proffered hand. "It's nice to be back."

"Hope you'll stick around. We could use all the financial geniuses we can get hold of."

"I always planned to come home. I was just waiting for the right time."

Bertie nodded. "No time like the present, as they say." With that, he wrapped an arm around his protesting wife and swept her out the door.

"I'm sorry about that," Annie murmured. "It's not true, you know."

"What's not true?"

"The part about Pops. He never thought you were interested in Pansy or Trish. Heck, Trish was still a kid when you…" She took a deep breath. Time to end the lies. Time to face what she'd done and own up to it. "When *I* had you thrown off the island."

He lifted his mug in acknowledgment of her admission. "Pansy thinks it's true. She must have gotten that impression from somewhere."

"She's just confused. Maybe it's all those hormones running riot. I remember during her last pregnancy she got it in her head that Bertie was going to leave her. She cried for six months straight. Nothing anyone said could convince her otherwise."

Sam's mood lightened somewhat. "I gather he didn't leave?"

"As if! The man's flat-out crazy about her." She grimaced. "He'd have to be to put up with all those tears.

I know I'd have been tempted beyond endurance to give her a good smack."

"Saint Annie strikes again?"

She chuckled. "There are times when Pansy can try the patience of a saint. That was one of them."

"So." He set his mug on the counter and faced her. "When do we start planning our wedding?"

Her mug slammed onto the counter beside his. "Excuse me?"

"You realize we may not have any choice if the hens get wind of last night's escapade." He checked his watch. "How long do you think it'll be before Bertie or Pansy spill the beans?"

"They won't say anything," Annie insisted confidently.

"You sure?"

"Bertie has a strong sense of honor. Once he thinks about it for a spell, he'll make sure Pansy keeps quiet. It may look like my dear sister rules the roost, but when he puts his foot down, no one argues. Not even Rolly."

That caught Sam's attention. "Now that I'd like to see."

"Stick around and you might." Which reminded her. "Were you serious about what you told Bertie? Are you really planning to stay?"

"Dead serious." She'd piled her hair on top of her head when she'd dressed and he plucked at the clip anchoring it there, grinning devilishly as her curls tumbled around her shoulders. "It'll give me plenty of time to take care of business. A whole lifetime, if necessary."

She swept her hair from her face. "Keep that up and I'll cut it off."

His amusement died. "Don't. It's too pretty to cut."

Was that why she never had? Because Sam liked it

long? When they'd started dating, he'd touch it cautiously, as though ready to pull back at the first sign she'd taken offense. Later, he'd gather it in his hands, twining the strands in his fingers. As a boy, he'd once explained, his mother had told him that an island woman who was part fairy had spun Annie's hair from straw into gold. For years he'd believed the fanciful tale. Finally, on her sixth birthday, he'd gotten up the nerve to find out for himself.

And though he'd discovered that day that her hair wasn't made from gold, he didn't mind. He still thought it was the prettiest color he'd ever seen. And, as he'd told her on more than one occasion, much softer than real gold would have been.

"So what now?" Annie asked cautiously. "You said you came back for Myrtle's sake, because she was worried about me. Personally, I think it was for revenge. Now you've told Pansy and Bertie you're going to stick around for a while."

"Not for a while. Permanently."

She nodded, accepting that she'd have a full measure of heartache to deal with over the coming months. Seeing Sam on a regular basis and watching as he integrated into island life would be difficult enough. But coming across him unexpectedly at Drake's Supermarket or at a local ball game, arriving home at Myrtle's and finding him sitting at her kitchen table with a cup of tea steaming in front of him... How would she bear it? Having, but not having.

"That still doesn't answer my question," she finally said.

"You mean...what am I going to do about you?"

She didn't like the sound of that. "Yes."

His grin reappeared. "Why, I continue to try and compromise you, of course."

"I'm serious," she snapped.

"So am I." He straightened. "Since Bertie and Pansy can't be counted on to do my dirty work for me, I'll just have to take care of it myself." He released a gusty sigh. "So much to do and so little time. Where are you headed today? If I'm going to get in a full measure of retribution, I'll have to know your plans."

"*You* are free to go where you want. *I* have a job to get to."

"Really? I thought teachers were off for the summer."

"I tutor high school students every July. Or rather, I do as soon as I can round them up."

"Round them up? Interesting. And where, Miss Bo-Peep, will you find your poor lost sheep?"

"This time of year?" She regarded him in amusement. "Are you kidding?"

"Ahh. The beach. How about if I lend a hand?"

"No, thanks. I can take care of it all by my lonesome."

"You sure?"

"Positive."

She didn't give him an opportunity to argue. Scooping up the keys to her...*his* motorcycle, she escaped out the door. Her growling stomach reminded her that she'd only breakfasted on a cup of coffee, which was far from sufficient. Too bad. She didn't dare return to the kitchen and face Sam again. He'd gotten too close today, slipped past barriers that were surprisingly shaky. After so many years they should have been more solid. She'd have to see what she could do about that.

Buzzing through town—and exceeding the speed limit out of sheer defiance—she wound her way toward the one small harbor Delacorte Island boasted. She kept a small outboard, *Lulubelle*, tied up there, a boat her grand-mother had given her on her sixteenth birthday. The mornings she was supposed to tutor, she'd take *Lulubelle* out to a small deserted island south of Delacorte, appro-priately nicknamed Point Doom. It was little more than an overgrown sandbar and during low tide people could actually wade to it. Surfers, in particular, liked how the waves broke there. Without a doubt, it was where she'd find her delinquent students.

Climbing aboard *Lulubelle*, she lowered the outboard engine into the water. It only took two yanks of the starter rope before the engine fired.

"Here, let me," Sam offered, appearing unexpectedly above her. He tossed off the lines that secured her to the dock and jumped on board. "Well?" he asked with an easy grin. "What are you waiting for?"

You, she almost admitted. Instead, she indulged in a single fierce frown, hoping it would disguise her exhilara-tion. "Sit down before you capsize us," she ordered. As soon as he'd settled himself in the bow, she grabbed the throttle arm and steered them sedately out of the harbor and toward the cut that connected the sound to the ocean.

"You know I almost lost you going through town," Sam commented.

"There's only one main road. I'd think that would make me a little hard to lose."

"Myrtle wasn't kidding. You really are reckless when you ride my bike. Keep it up and I'm going to take my keys back." He didn't give her a chance to argue. "So where are we going?"

"Point Doom."

Sam shook his head. "They won't be there."

"Why not?"

"It's high tide and the wind's out of the northeast.

They'll be on the north shore. The action's better there today."

"We'll see." Ten minutes later, wrestling the craft through surprisingly choppy seas, Annie realized Sam was right. Point Doom was completely deserted, its connection to Delacorte severed by the swift currents of an incoming tide. "Guess we'd better head in. The surf's too rough for poor *Lulubelle*. That hurricane stalled off the Florida coast must be kicking up the waves."

"It's too pretty a day to go back. Why don't you take us into the sound and circle around to Myrtle's. It'll be smoother there."

"I don't have the time. I have lessons to give, remember?"

"I'm sure your students won't object to a couple hours' delay."

"They might not, but—" The engine gave a little sputter before catching again. "Uh-oh."

Sam's gaze sharpened. "You low on gas?"

"I just filled it yesterday."

"Where's your spare gas can?"

"I…ah…don't have it with me." A cardinal sin, if ever there was one.

"Why the hell not?"

"Because I just filled the tank yesterday." The engine sputtered again, giving lie to her claim.

"You're always supposed to carry spare gas." He looked around. "Where are the oars?"

Another sin she'd have to confess. "I loaned them to Pansy."

"Dammit, Annie! Steer toward the point. Maybe there's enough gas left to get us there."

There wasn't. They stalled several hundred feet shy of their destination. The current caught the small boat, pushing it away from the island. Breakers slapped the hull, threatening to swamp them.

"We'll have to swim for it," Sam said.

"No," Annie protested. "I'm not leaving *Lulubelle* to fend for herself! She might swallow too much water and drown."

"I wasn't planning on abandoning her." Without another word, he kicked off his sneakers, yanked his shirt over his head and executed a quick dive into the water. "Toss me the bowline," he requested as soon as he surfaced.

She threw it to him and slipped off her sandals, as well. "Hang on. I'll be right there."

"Stay in the boat."

"Sam, you can't tow us by yourself. It's too far and the current's too strong." She didn't bother arguing. With the ease of long habit, she dived into the ocean, bobbing up just in time to get smacked by an incoming wave. She choked on the briny water.

Sam grabbed her arm and held her up. "You're not going to do *Lulubelle* much good if I have to let go of her to rescue you."

"I don't need rescuing!"

"Honey, I've never met anyone more in need of rescuing than you. Now if you plan to help, grab the rope with me and let's start kicking."

It took a full forty minutes of hard swimming to reach the narrow islet. The high tide had almost covered it, leaving little more than a hump of sand sticking out of the water. Waves broke over the top, threatening to sweep Annie's feet out from under her. Panting, her arms and legs feeling more like rubber than bone and muscle, she helped Sam run the boat aground. Then she flopped down on the sand next to him.

"Now what do we do?" she asked.

"Looks like we only have one option."

"Wait for someone to come along and rescue us?"

"Nope."

"I'm not swimming back to the island." She slanted him a warning look. "And neither are you."

"Wasn't planning on swimming back."

Exhaustion made her cranky. "Exactly what *were* you planning?"

He fixed her with a gimlet stare. "Just as soon as I catch my breath, I plan to ruin the hell out of you."

CHAPTER FIVE

SAM waited, curious to see Annie's reaction to his statement. For a long moment, she simply stared at him, her blue eyes wide with a mixture of apprehension and hunger. She looked like a beached mermaid confronted by a lusty pirate. Her hair, as rich a gold as Spanish doubloons, tumbled down her back and shoulders, the tangle of wet strands binding her arms to her sides in ropes of silk. The skirt of her peach-colored dress swirled about her thighs as another breaker raced up the hump of sand to foam around them. He liked her in cotton, especially after a good soaking. The semitransparent material clung, offering him a glimpse of paradise.

"You can't ruin me," she finally said. "Someone might see."

He nodded solemnly. "People are supposed to see, sweetheart. Or at least find out. That's sort of the point of a good ruination."

"But you can't," she protested.

A smile played across his mouth. "And why not?"

"Because I'm a schoolteacher."

Right. It made perfect sense. "Schoolteachers are immune to seduction? Gee, I never realized that."

"Well, sure. It's a law or something."

"We wouldn't want to break the law, now would we?"

She shook her head, but he didn't think she looked too certain. It was a good sign. "It probably wouldn't be the best idea."

"You're forgetting two small problems."

"What are those?"

"First, I'm a Beaumont."

"And that makes you immune to the law?"

"It sure does."

"And second?"

"I promised to compromise you."

Was that a hopeful gleam in her eye? "And you never break your promises."

"Never." Another wave broke over them and this time her skirt swirled around her hips. It was more temptation than he could stand. He allowed the rush of water to carry him into her arms. "This is the second time I've gotten lucky," he teased.

To his relief, she didn't attempt to push him away but permitted him to anchor her close. Though considering her hair bound them together in a silken net, he didn't see that she had much choice. "What do you mean?"

"First my bedroom. Now we have this deserted beach just begging for a good frolic. It looks like the fates are working against you, sweetheart."

For a brief instant, she regarded him with serious eyes. Then the corners crinkled and she smiled in a way that stopped his breath. So poignant. So mysterious. So filled with longing and regret. What he chose to focus on, though, was the tiny spark of desire lurking in their blue depths. It was a reluctant wanting, he didn't doubt that for a minute. But it was there and he intended to take full advantage of that fact.

He framed her face, giving her ample time to try to change his mind. The sun kissed her cheeks while the sky painted her eyes with the intensity of its color. Her lips were damp with sea spray. He'd taste the ocean's salty tears on them when he kissed her. Taste it, too, along the sweep of her neck and on the budding tips of her breasts.

A tumble of water lifted them, gently tossing them higher on the shore before washing them clean of sand as it receded. Overhead, a laughing gull dipped low to confirm they hadn't brought along bread crumbs to share. Not finding anything of interest, it tacked on the wind and wheeled from view.

"You know what's going to happen, don't you?" he asked, shading her from the sun's rays with his body.

"I believe, Mr. Beaumont, that you're going to do your level best to seduce me."

"That's exactly what I plan to do, Miss Delacorte." He lifted an eyebrow. "Are you going to resist?"

Laughter blossomed within her gaze. "Maybe just a little."

"You don't look too worried."

"Oh, I'm not."

"Why not?"

"Because it's you, Sam." So guileless, so certain. More certain than he was, that was for damned sure.

"And why does that make a difference?"

The amusement faded, replaced by more regrets than any one person should ever have to bear. "Unlike most men who've been hurt, you're not one to hit back."

Anger rippled through him. "You're kidding yourself, princess."

She shook her head. "Anyone else I'd keep as far away from as I could."

"But not me?"

"Not you. You might try to make good your threat. But..." She broke off, catching her bottom lip between her teeth.

"Go on. Finish it."

"But somehow you'll make sure I don't get hurt in the process." Her brows drew together. "I know it doesn't make any sense."

"No sense at all. Shall I show you how wrong you are?"

"You can try."

He wouldn't get a better offer. He lowered his head, surprised when she met him halfway. She tasted of salt, just as he'd expected. But he hadn't anticipated the heat or the way he'd want to use her mouth, first penetrating, taking her with hard, consuming bites. Next to snatch a gentle nibble, teasing, playing with the swollen fullness of her lips. And then to take them slowly. Languid and moist and thorough, her mouth was as ripe with passion as it was raw with hunger.

The wave came back, hitting them hard, flinging her skirt to her waist. He took it as an invitation and rolled between her legs. Sliding his hands beneath her, he filled his palms and urged her close, showing her how nature had designed them to fit together. Her knees clamped around his hips and she whispered his name, the husky sound carried off on a tropical breeze.

"Are you seduced yet?" he demanded.

She closed her eyes, her breath escaping in a soft moan. "I'd say I was a single wave away from utter ruination."

"I'd say you were right."

He turned his attention to her dress. Buttons slipped through buttonholes almost of their own accord. And then Sam eased the edges of her dress apart. She was so beautiful, her breasts pale and full, the tips beaded from the ocean. Unable to resist, he seared them with a kiss. Her back arched instinctively and her fingers dug deep into the sand. She was open to him, offering herself in the sweetest of surrenders. His revenge was at hand. All he had to do was strip away the bit of cotton that was her final barricade and she'd be his.

He hesitated, more torn than he'd ever been in his life. With a reluctant groan, he rested his head on a heavenly cushion and silently cursed himself for a fool. Annie was right. How the hell had she known? He couldn't hurt her. Nor could he break the vow he'd made to himself when they'd first started dating. A vow that demanded he take her to wife before he took her to bed.

"I've made a decision, Annie."

He could hear her heart pounding against his cheek. "What decision?"

"You can keep your sign up for a little longer."

Her fingers slipped through his hair. "You're not ready to keep your promise?"

"Not quite yet."

"You might not get another opportunity," she warned.

"Oh, I suspect I will." A breaker tumbled over them, cooling their heated skin. "I expect I'll have years and years of opportunities."

Before she could reply, a shout drifted across the open water toward them. "There they are!" There was no mistaking the voice. It was Mayor Pike.

"Hurry, boys, before it's too late."

"Rolly, sit the hell down. You're gonna flip us over. And leave that gun where it's at. I don't know what it is with you and that pistol, but I'm beginning to think you have a fixation or something."

"I'm the sheriff, dammit all! I'm supposed to have a weapon fixation. Watch where you're steering this tub, Pike. You're about to run us aground."

"Durn it all, Rolly. I'm telling you to plant yourself on that seat. If I run us aground, it'll be due to your backside blocking my blasted view. Now, who's jumping overboard after Annie? Ben, you're sitting there with nothing to do. Go get her.''

"But…she's…she's—"

"She's what? Spit it out, Ben."

"She's got her dress all in a twist."

"Well, what the hell are you waitin' for, boy?" Rolly roared. "Haul your can overboard and get that Beaumont away from her before he has that dress twisted right off."

Sam heaved a sigh and helped Annie to her feet. "Looks like you've been rescued again."

Delicious color stained her cheeks. "Stand in front of me while I get my dress buttoned up," she pleaded.

"That's what I planned, sweetheart. No matter what I said, it wasn't my intention for anyone else to see you compromised. Just me." He gave her a minute, then glanced over his shoulder. "How's it coming?"

"Darn it all, Sam. Everything's wet. And sandy. And I'm having the devil's own luck getting these buttons done up. Do you suppose the salt water shrank the holes?"

Suppressing a grin, he pretended to ponder the matter. "As I recall, cotton does shrink. So I suppose it's possible." He risked another quick look and promptly wished he'd resisted. If Ben weren't swimming steadily toward him, they'd be frolicking in the surf again. "Need some help?"

"No! What I need is your promise that you won't unbutton me anymore."

He frowned. "Gee, honey, I'm not sure I can do that."

"Try!"

"You know I'm a man of my word. If I give a promise like that, I'm obligated to stick to it."

"Which is exactly why you're going to make this one.

Now say it, Sam Beaumont. Promise you won't unbutton me again.''

"Tell you what. I'll promise not to unbutton you the next time we're in this sort of predicament. How's that?''

"Not good enough. I wasn't planning on being in this sort of predicament ever again.''

"I assume that means you'll bring a spare can of gas with you on your next outing with *Lulubelle*?'' He wasn't joking any longer and hoped his tone conveyed as much.

"Trust me. I've learned my lesson on that score.''

"And your oars?''

"I'll pick them up from Pansy later today.''

"Fair enough.''

"What about your promise?''

He simply grinned. "You almost done with those buttons, Annie? Ben's getting mighty close. Lucky for you he's such a slow swimmer.''

"I can't get the top two,'' she wailed.

"Guess the Musketeers are in for a treat, then.''

"Sam! You haven't promised.''

"Tell you what. I'll promise not to unbutton any of your dresses for…oh, how does a week sound?''

"Not nearly as good as a month.''

"Sorry, sweetheart,'' he apologized, not sounding the least regretful. "A week's the best I can offer.''

"Fine. A week. But I'm holding you to that, Sam.''

"I'm sure you will. Just as you can be sure I'll do my damnedest to talk you out of it.''

"Not a chance.''

"We'll see.''

Ben tromped up the sand toward them, ending their discussion. He eyed them warily. "Hey there, you two.''

To Sam's amusement, Annie offered her most saintly smile. He also noticed that Ben carefully kept his gaze away from her drooping neckline, though he must have noticed the problem since ruddy color tinted his cheeks. "Oh, hello, Ben. Fancy running into you here," she said, using her best parlor manners.

"Is there a problem, Miss Annie?"

"Why, yes, now that you mention it. There is."

Ben glanced uneasily at Sam. "Something I..." He threw a quick look over his shoulder at the boat containing a glowering Mayor Pike and Sheriff Rolly. Reassured, he addressed them again. "I mean, is there anything *we* can do for you?"

"How kind." She flipped her hair over her shoulder, apparently realized how it drew attention to her unbuttoned dress and just as quickly flipped it back to help fill in the gap. Sam was willing to bet a week's salary she'd start wearing a bra from now on. What a shame. "I'm embarrassed to admit it, but I ran out of gas."

Sam snorted. "You should have tried for something more original, sweetheart. Like water in the fuel line. Or a broken prop."

She turned on him in a flash. "Ben's not stupid, you know. He can see full well the prop isn't broken."

"Somehow I doubt he'd have called you on it." He slanted Ben a look of inquiry. "Would you?"

"No sirree. I surely wouldn't."

Sam nodded. "Thought not." He addressed Annie again. "But perhaps the clogged fuel line would have been a better bet. No one could come right out and call you a liar with that one."

"Why should I lie?" She must have forgotten about the buttons because she whipped her hair over her shoulder, smacking poor Ben across the chops. Not that she noticed what she'd done. Or the way the poor man tumbled back into the water. "We *did* run out of gas."

"You know...I've been meaning to ask you about that. If you wanted to get me alone, all you had to do was ask. You didn't need to go setting up this elaborate charade."

"That's *it*!" She spun on her heel. "Ben...what the heck are you doing in the water?"

He splashed ashore. "I...ah...tripped."

"Well, come over here and help me pull *Lulubelle* off this sandbar. We can tie her to the mayor's boat for a tow in."

"Sure thing, Miss Annie. Anything you say."

"I want to go home. Now." She must have finally heard how churlish she sounded because her eyes widened in dismay. "I mean...if it wouldn't be too much trouble?" She offered another of her sugary smiles.

"No, ma'am. Happy to help." He circled her warily. "You leaving, too, Sam?"

"I've pretty much accomplished all I could under the circumstances." He grinned. If Saint Annie's back got any stiffer, it would snap. "Unless there's something more I can do for you, Miss Delacorte?"

She gave *Lulubelle* a good, hard shove toward the sea. "Not unless drowning yourself is on the list. It would sure save me the trouble."

By the time they'd safely moored at the dock, all Annie wanted was to climb into a shower and never leave. Instead, she hopped onto Sam's old motorcycle, crammed her helmet over her sand-and-salt-crusted hair and flew through town toward home, her damp skirts flapping around her legs. She didn't need to look in her side mirror to know that Sam was hot on her tail.

"I warned you," he started in on her the instant they arrived at Myrtle's. "I warned you what I'd do if you didn't slow down. Since the law doesn't seem interested in stopping you, looks like I'll have to.'' He thrust out his hand, palm up. "Give them to me.''

She retreated a step. "Give you what?''

"My keys, as you damned well know.''

"And if I refuse?''

"Then I'll take them from you.''

A low, husky chuckle came from the porch behind them. "Hell, Sam. Don't tell me you returned home just to scare little girls and take away their toys?''

Annie spun around and stared at one of the most striking women she'd ever seen. Her hair was as dark as Sam's, only shorter, brushed back at the sides and spiked on top. On anyone else, such a hairstyle would have looked ridiculous. But somehow this woman had the panache to carry it off. She sauntered down the porch steps—at least Annie assumed it was sauntering. It certainly looked like a saunter. But whatever that particular walk was, it drew instant attention to her endless legs, legs topped by a minuscule skirt. Vivid green eyes appraised Annie every bit as carefully as Annie appraised her.

She had to be a nasty, man-eating witch, Annie decided. Of course, another word offered itself as a potential substitute for "witch.'' But the town saint wasn't supposed to have such uncharitable thoughts, which caused her no end of grief when they insisted on leaping into her head.

But, really! Why else would the woman have shown up at this precise moment? Somehow she knew Annie would happen along, reeking of fish from Mayor Pike's boat and wearing a sand-encrusted cotton dress that was busily shrink-wrapping itself around her with each passing second. Not to mention dripping salt water from long, stringy, wind-whipped hair. And why hadn't she thought to do spikes instead of a silly purple stripe when it was perfectly apparent that Sam adored spikes? At least then she wouldn't be dripping all over the place.

"I take that back," the woman said, taking due note of Annie's gaping bodice. "Not such a little girl after all." She slanted those wicked green eyes in Sam's direction. "You dirty dog."

"Well, well. Look what the cat dragged in." Sam grabbed the woman and swung her around, giving her an enthusiastic kiss on the cheek. "What are you doing here, Diana?"

"Hello, lover." The greeting had to be deliberate, a zinger that successfully hit its intended mark. Annie glanced over her shoulder, expecting to find a big fat bull's-eye plastered to her shrink-wrapped backside. "I was just passing through so thought I'd drop in and see how you were doing."

Her accent betrayed her New York origins, which gave lie to her story. Delacorte Island wasn't on the way to anywhere. Delacorte Island was the end of a destination, not a stopover point. Annie folded her arms across her chest and waited for Sam to call the woman a flat-out liar. Instead, he laughed. "I'm glad you did." He turned to Annie. "Diana Starr, meet Annie Delacorte. Diana's my partner."

The woman had the unmitigated gall to smile pleasantly and offer her hand. As if! "Soon to be ex-partner, unless I can talk him out of it," she confessed.

Ex-partner? That perked Annie up some, at least enough for her to shake hands and bare her teeth in what she hoped would pass for a smile. "I'm so very pleased to meet you," she said in a voice that dripped honey. Southern women excelled at that, offering a bit of sugar so their victims wouldn't notice the knife sticking out of their backs. And Annie was no exception despite being branded a saint.

Beside her, Sam snorted. "Don't get too close, Diana. She's not as harmless as she looks."

"Is she the one, then?"

"Yup. She's the one."

"One what?" Annie asked suspiciously.

"The one who has an entire island named for her family," Diana lied gracefully. "It's a beautiful place."

"We think so."

Diana turned to Sam and slipped her hand through his arm. "Listen, hon. I don't have a lot of time and I've already spent most of it tracking you down. We need to talk."

"Sure. Why don't we go over to my place. I can show you around and you can do all the talking since I suspect I'll be doing all the listening."

She chuckled. "Perfect." Turning to Annie, she offered another charming smile. "I'm glad we had a chance to meet."

"That makes one—I mean two of us." Annie worked on offering a friendly expression. But with salt crystals caking her skin, it was tough. Salt always made her pucker. "If you'll excuse me, I'm in desperate need of a shower."

"A boating accident?" Diana asked sympathetically.

"We ran out of gas."

The New York chippy chuckled. "I gather when you run out of gas in a boat, you're forced to swim to the nearest gas station?"

Witch! "Oh, no," Annie retorted blithely. "I just hitch a ride on the first dolphin that swims by. Island girls are taught the knack at an early age."

Sam winced. "I think that's our cue to go." He dropped an arm around Diana's shoulders and urged her toward a rental car parked beneath a nearby mimosa.

Realizing it was her cue, too, Annie stamped toward the house. Why hadn't anyone taught her how to saunter? It would have come in real handy about now. Of course, with stiff, wet cotton glued to her skin it would have been a bit of a challenge. But at least she'd have made a graceful exit.

"Oh, Annie?"

She spun around so fast she made herself dizzy. "Yes?"

"Tell Myrtle I might not be back for dinner."

And with that, Sam and his silk-clad soon-to-be-ex-partner climbed into the car, leaving Annie muttering more of those words that would bring a quick end to her sainthood if she ever muttered them where someone actually heard.

"You don't understand, Aunt Myrtle."

The older woman glanced up from her knitting. "What don't I understand, dear?"

Annie paced to the window and stared out at the night sky. "Sam's trying to seduce me. He's admitted as much."

"I'm sure he's just teasing. He always was a mischievous boy."

"No! It's more than that. He wants revenge because I…" The words caught in her throat and she gripped the sill. "Because I—"

"Asked the Musketeers to intervene on your behalf seven years ago?"

Annie's shoulders slumped. "You heard about it?"

"Really, Annie. How can you ask a question like that?

It's common knowledge. Secrets don't keep on Delacorte Island. You should know that by now."

"You'd have thought so," she muttered.

Myrtle's knitting needles clicked for a time. "I also know that your bags were packed to go that night," she mentioned sedately.

Uh-oh. Annie turned around. "Where... ?"

"Pansy mentioned it."

Blast Pansy and her big mouth. "What else did my dear sister say?"

"That you and Joe had an unholy row."

Annie returned to her chair and perched on the edge. "Pops found out I was going to run off with Sam," she explained.

"Hmm." Myrtle dropped her knitting onto her lap. "I can understand him being a trifle upset."

"He's always hated Beaumonts." Annie shot the older woman an apologetic look. "Not you, I'm sure," she lied.

"Oh, yes. He hated me, too."

Good grief! Was there nothing Myrtle hadn't uncovered? Annie's eyes widened in alarm. Surely she didn't know the rest. "What else did Pansy tell you? Did she say what the fight was about?"

Myrtle's regard intensified. "I thought you said it was over your eloping with Sam."

Annie sighed. Maybe she should take up knitting. It would give her hands something to do other than twist together in her lap and betray her. "Yes. Of course."

"Joe must have said something quite horrible to keep you from going with Sam. I know for a fact you loved him very much."

More twisting. "Pops convinced me to wait."

"Now you've waited. Seven whole years." Myrtle

picked up her cane and nudged Annie with the tip. "So? Why haven't you made things up with him?"

"I told you. He's not interested in making up. He's interested in revenge."

Myrtle snorted. "Oh, stuff and nonsense. Say you're sorry. Give him a hug and a kiss and he'll come around."

I've already done that, she was tempted to confess. "And if that doesn't work?"

"Then you tell him the real reason you didn't go with him that night."

Annie froze. "What do you mean?"

"You can't fool me, missy. I know Joe Delacorte better than you might think. He said something to you that night."

She shook her head. "No."

"He said something that stopped you from going." A strange sadness flickered within the depths of her dark eyes. "And I'm telling you that if you want to work things out with Sam, you'll tell him what it was."

"I can't," Annie whispered.

"Yes, my dear, you can. And you will."

Myrtle didn't know what Pops had said or she'd never have offered that advice. "I'm not going to marry Sam."

The knitting needles resumed their clicking. "You'll have to tell him eventually. You'll save yourself a lot of heartache if you do it now."

"I'll...I'll think about it."

Not that thinking about it would change her mind. Because though everything Myrtle had said was the truth, there was one small problem. It wasn't her secret. And she'd sooner take whatever revenge Sam deemed appropriate than betray those who'd be hurt by her revelation. Of course, it wasn't her honor that she'd be sacrificing with her silence.

It was her happiness.

"I just don't know what it is with women these days," Myrtle muttered.

"Excuse me?"

Shards of light flashed off the knitting needles. "If I were you, I'd track that man down this very minute, rip that black-haired harpy out of his arms and say what needs to be said."

Annie blinked in surprise. "You think I should?"

"I think you'd better. And I'd be right quick about it, too."

Annie caught the implication. She glanced out the window again. It was late. Far too late for Sam and Diana to still be talking. Maybe she should take Myrtle's suggestion, or at least the tracking and ripping part. She wouldn't mind that in the least. And if she neglected to accomplish the rest? Well, these things happened.

"I think I'll take my bike for a little spin."

Myrtle smiled complacently. "I thought you might."

"Is there anything I can say that will change your mind? Anything at all?"

"Sorry, Diana. Not a thing."

"A pity." She wandered to the open window and looked out. "Nice view."

Sam braced his shoulder against the casing, wishing a hotheaded blonde stood beside him instead of a savvy brunette. "Annie said more or less the same thing the last time she was in here."

Diana swiveled to face him. "Really?" she asked with a startled laugh. "You two...in here? I assumed from her sign—"

"Oh, her sign's still valid enough."

"You must be losing your touch," she teased lightly.

"You had the love of your life in your bedroom and nothing happened?"

"Oh, plenty happened. Just not that."

She lifted an eyebrow. "Do tell."

"The wind blew the door shut so hard the knobs fell off and trapped us in here."

"How...awkward." Her gaze swept past him to the door in question. "I assume you fixed the problem."

"Oh, yeah. I fixed it. Why?"

"Because the door's—" A resounding crash echoed through the house. "About to slam," she finished with a wince.

"Well, at least we don't have to worry about—" The knob hit the floor with a familiar clang. "Aw, hell."

"You were saying?" she asked dryly. "I thought you told me you fixed the problem."

He glared at the knob. "I did! I spent a full day on it."

"I hate to tell you this, Sam. But you make a much better Wall Street whiz than a mechanic."

"Repairman."

She shrugged. "Whatever. So now what? How do we get out of here?"

"If you were Annie, you'd jump out the window."

Diana burst out laughing. "Did she really?"

He lifted his right hand. "So help me."

"And if I'd rather not take such extreme measures?"

"You couldn't, even if you were so inclined," he admitted. "I trimmed the tree back from the house so she wouldn't be tempted into similar heroics anytime in the near future."

A shapely brow winged upward. "You mean, assuming you ever got her up here again, had the door blow shut and your newly repaired knobs pop off,'' she said in a wry voice.

She didn't miss a trick. "Yeah. Assuming all that."

"So now what?"

He eyed first the bed, then the chair. Damn. He crossed to the chair and lowered himself gingerly onto the seat. "Now we make ourselves comfortable and wait. I expect someone will show up eventually. Someone always does."

Unfortunately, rescue didn't arrive for several hours and it came in a form he least wanted to see.

"Sam? Are you here? Sam Beaumont, where the heck are you!"

He swore beneath his breath. "We're here, Annie. In the bedroom."

"Where...?" Feet pelted up the steps. "Sam Beaumont, you son of drunken sea cook!"

"Yes, sweetheart?"

"Don't you sweetheart me," she shouted. "Are you trapped in there with that woman?"

He closed his eyes and groaned. Great. Just great. "Sure am."

There was dead silence for a full minute. Then a fist impacted the door. Or maybe it was a foot. It was hard to tell. "Damn you, Sam Beaumont! You've gone and ruined the wrong woman! How could you?"

CHAPTER SIX

"ANNIE, could we discuss this later?" he requested. "Like after you help us get out of here?"

"Why should I? I think I'll call the Three Musketeers and let them rescue you. Maybe I'll even wait until tomorrow so she's ruined good and proper."

"Annie Delacorte! I swear, if you don't stick that knob in the door right this minute, I'll fall out of that tree and come after you. See if I don't."

"Hah! Now there's a sight I'd pay good money to witness."

"You just might have the opportunity."

"Children," Diana interrupted with a long-suffering sigh. "Please. This really isn't necessary."

"You don't understand," Annie said dolefully.

Were those tears he heard? Dammit all! Why couldn't he be where he could see her? Touch her and hold her? Console her with a kiss? Before he could reassure her, Diana waved him silent.

"What don't I understand, Annie?" she asked.

"He promised. He promised to ruin me and instead he ruined you."

"Annie?" Diana's voice was surprisingly gentle.

"Yes?"

"You have my word—nothing happened."

"You don't understand," she repeated. "It doesn't matter what you say. I might believe you. But you've been locked up in there with Sam for heaven knows how long." She sniffed. "I'm sure you're a very nice person, but you're not a saint. Everyone will believe you've been ruined. Sam has a reputation for that sort of thing. He's really quite good at it.''

Diana chuckled. ''Honey, I was ruined long ago. I think you'll find it's sort of like a broken dish. Everyone has a fit the first time it breaks, but they don't even notice when it gets dropped the second time.''

''Listen to her, Annie. Burnt toast can't be turned back into fresh bread. No offense, Diana.''

''None taken, lover. Now that we have that cleared up, would you mind letting us out of here, Miss Delacorte?''

''Just a sec. I'm looking for the knob. I do apologize, Diana. I really don't know what got into me.'' She sniffed again. ''I'm usually not so unfriendly. It's just—''

''I understand completely. Would you mind looking a little faster? Sam said the last ferry leaves at ten and my rental car and I would like to be on it.''

Sam groaned. ''I know what you're thinking, Annie. Don't you dare say it.''

''Whatever do you mean?''

Oh, yeah. She was using her sweet, Southern belle voice. It was a dead giveaway. ''Don't try that one on me. Don't say what you were thinking.''

''About not wanting her to miss her ferry?''

''That's the one. You really need to work on those unsaintly thoughts.''

She sighed. ''I'm well aware of that. I found the knob, by the way.''

''I'll put my end in first. You put yours in next and very gently turn the knob. Okay?''

''I think I can handle it.''

''Sarcasm, Annie?''

''Why, yes. I believe it was.''

An instant later, the door swung open and Diana sauntered out. "You people have very odd ways of entertaining yourselves." Her green eyes glittered with laughter. "It's been amusing, girls and boys, but I think I'll run along and leave you to your fun and games. I assume, Miss Delacorte, that you can give Sam a lift home?"

"I'll take care of him." If her smile was any sweeter, it would kill. "Thanks for coming."

"I wouldn't have missed it for the world."

"I'll be in touch," Sam told her, giving her another hug and kiss. He murmured something in her ear to which she grinned and nodded. As she started down the steps, he turned his attention to Annie. In another moment they'd be alone, and he waited for that knowledge to occur to her, as well. It didn't take long.

Her eyes grew wide and she edged toward the steps. "I think I've done all I can for one night."

"You mean caused all the trouble you can."

"Hey! I wasn't the one who got locked in the bedroom for the second time in two days." She gave him a pointed look. "Now there's an interesting coincidence."

Anger stirred. "What's that supposed to mean?"

"Gee, I don't know. Let's see. Two different women both trapped in your bedroom using the same clever scheme." She glared. "You figure it out."

"Are you suggesting I locked us in there on purpose?" he demanded in disbelief.

"Are you claiming you didn't?" Wisely, she didn't wait for an answer but scampered down the steps.

Not that he'd let her get away with it. He charged down the stairs after her. "Don't even think about leaving without me," he called.

"No problem," she snapped over her shoulder. "I won't give it a single thought. I'll just do it."

Not if he could help it. She raced for the waiting motorcycle and hopped aboard. But in the few seconds it took her to rev the engine, he slid on behind her and wrapped his arms around her waist. Last time they'd ridden together, she'd been the one in back, encasing his hips with her silken thighs. Now he returned the favor, cupping her snugly between his legs and spreading his hands across the flat planes of her belly.

"Take me for a ride," he whispered in her ear.

She didn't need further prompting. Gunning the engine, she sped down his drive, avoiding potholes with the ease of long practice. Did she realize how revealing that was? To be so deft, she must have visited Soundings on a regular basis. At least, frequently enough to know the vagaries of his driveway after dark.

They gained the main road running through town and her speed picked up, kicking her hair into his face. The silken strands whipped against his cheeks and he inhaled the sweet scent of her shampoo, knowing he should make her return to Myrtle's for their helmets. Knowing, too, that he should have her slow down. But he didn't want to slow down any more than she did. He wanted speed. He wanted a strong, balmy breeze cooling his heated skin. And he wanted to feel the powerful rumble of the Harley vibrate through him, echoing the hot pounding in his veins.

She nudged the speed up a notch and he tapped her shoulder. "Enough, sweetheart. Slow it down."

He didn't think she'd listen, but then he heard the reluctant checking of the engine at the same instant as he caught the flash of blue light reflecting in her side mirrors. Damn. Any other time, he'd have been thrilled to see the law officials of Delacorte Island do their duty. But just this once, he'd have been quite happy to have them ignore Annie's excesses.

She glanced over her shoulder toward the patrol car following them and he saw her mouth a word that caused him to grin. "You've done it now, princess."

"Don't worry. It's just Bertie. Now listen, Sam. Don't say anything to provoke him. He and I have gone through this drill before. He'll give me a good chewing out about going so fast. I'll act all pitiful and apologetic. And we'll be on our way in no time. Okay?"

"Whatever you say," he agreed with a shrug. It should be interesting to watch her in action, if nothing else.

Stopping along a deserted strip of road, she waited until Bertie came up beside them. "Hey there, Bertie," she greeted him cheerfully.

"Good evening, Miss Delacorte. Would you step off your motorcycle, please? You, too, Mr. Beaumont."

"Miss Delacorte? Mr. Beaumont?" she asked with a laugh, climbing off the bike. "That's a new one."

"Yes, ma'am. May I see your license and registration, please?"

"My…" She frowned. "What's got into you, Bertie? You know I never carry that stuff with me. It's in my purse at Myrtle's."

"Yes, ma'am. So you admit you're driving without a license?"

"Well…sure." She stared in bewilderment. "What's with this 'ma'am' business?"

He cleared his throat. "Just being polite."

And by the book, Sam realized. Their situation just got a whole lot more interesting. He propped his hip on the bike, prepared to be entertained.

"Miss Delacorte, are you aware driving without a license in your possession is against the law?"

"Good grief, Bertie! *No one* on Delacorte carries their license on them unless they're going off-island. It might get lost or wet or snapped up by a fish or something. Why don't you tell me what's—''

"I see you're also operating your motorcycle without a helmet.''

It finally dawned on her that matters weren't going quite as expected. "I'm real sorry about that, Bertie,'' she offered contritely. "You know I'm normally extra careful about that. But this time I was in a bit of a hurry and—''

"Yes, ma'am. I was getting to that. Were you aware that your speed was well in excess of the posted limit?''

So much for contrition. She planted her hands on her hips and glared at him. "It usually is, Bertie, but you've never—''

"It might be more appropriate if you call me Deputy Hinkle for the time being.''

She blinked, her mouth opening and closing like a landed fish. "You want me to call my own brother-in-law Deputy—''

"Hinkle. Yes, ma'am.''

"Bertram Hinkle, have you lost your ever blessed mind?''

"Excuse me?''

"Have you gone crazy?'' She turned to Sam. "He's gone plumb crazy. It must be the stress of Pansy's pregnancy. I told you what a hard time she gave him during the last one.'' She faced Bertie again. "What's she up and done, Bert—I mean, Deputy? Maybe I can help. Do you need a good, home-cooked meal? Is that it? How about a baby-sitter so you and Pansy can have a night on the town?''

"Ma'am? I believe you've just tried to bribe an officer of the law. I'm afraid I'm going to have to take you in.''

"*What!*" She struggled for breath. "What the heck for?"

"Speeding. Driving without a license. Riding a motorcycle without a helmet. And attempted bribery. Would you please place your hands on top of your head and turn around."

"You have got to be joking. At least you damn well better be joking!"

Perhaps it was time to step in, Sam decided. "Er...Deputy?"

"Sir, I advise you not to interfere with my arrest. To do so will force me to arrest you, too." He looked at Sam hopefully. "Will you be interfering?"

"Abso-damn-lutely," he answered promptly.

"I see, sir. Please turn around and place your hands on your head, as well."

"You're going to handcuff both of us?" Sam asked, curious to see how Bertie intended to proceed from here.

"I'm afraid I'll have to handcuff you to each other since I only have one set of cuffs."

Sam grinned. "Got it."

Before Annie could protest, Bertie snapped on the cuffs, shackling them together. Sam fought to hide his amusement. Somebody had to have put him up to this. Pansy, perhaps, or even Myrtle. Well, fine. He'd play along.

"What now, Deputy?"

"Now I'll have to take you in."

Bertie escorted them to his patrol car and helped them into the back seat. All he got for his efforts was a nonstop tongue-blistering from Annie. She threw in a few of her less-than-saintly words, which managed to turn poor Bertie's ears a bright shade of pink. Switching off his flashing lights, he executed a quick U-turn and headed toward town.

To Sam's surprise, the police station was deserted except for a lonely dispatcher. Since there were only two policemen on the entire island, it meant that Rolly had turned in for the evening.

"I'm not going to process you until tomorrow," Bertie said, showing the first hint of nervousness he'd displayed all evening. "I need to wait and see if Rolly plans to press charges."

"You mean you're going to lock us up until morning?" Annie demanded, outraged. "What about our phone call? What about my fingerprints?"

Bertie's professional demeanor vanished like fog in the sun. "Now, Annie," he attempted to placate, "you wouldn't want to wake Myrtle at this hour. You can give her a call first thing in the morning. And fingerprinting you will get ink all over your hands. You wouldn't like it one little bit. That stuff's a pain to wash off."

He urged them toward the back of the station and the jail cells. All two of them. The first was filled with boxes.

"We haven't gotten around to unpacking our new computer equipment just yet," Bertie explained before waving them into the other cell. "So I'll have to put you both in together."

The door clanged shut behind them. "What about the handcuffs?" Sam asked.

"I'll...ah...be along to collect those in a little while."

Sam bit off a laugh. "Right. No hurry."

"No hurry!" Annie protested, her voice rising an octave. "How can you say that?"

"Relax, sweetheart. I don't expect we'll be in here for long."

She grabbed the bars of the jail cell, practically jerking

his arm from the socket. "I don't understand. What in the world has gotten into Bertie?"

"I suspect your antics have pushed him as far as he cares to be pushed."

"Antics?" She glared at him. "What antics?"

"Come on, Annie." He gently disengaged her fingers from the bars. "You know what I mean. First your speeding and now riding without your helmet. You've gotten too reckless and this is his way of stopping you."

"But why involve you?"

He had his suspicions about that, too, but decided to keep them to himself. "Probably because he knew I'd raise hell once he arrested you," he offered as an alternate excuse. "I'm guessing he threw me in with you so I couldn't rout Rolly out of bed."

Her bewildered expression tied his gut in a knot. "Do you really think we'll be stuck in here all night?"

"Maybe." At her crestfallen expression, he wrapped his free arm around her. "I doubt we'll be locked up that long," he reassured her. "The dispatcher saw what was going on. My guess is she'll alert Rolly for us."

Annie looked around, her unease clearly apparent. "What do we do in the meantime?"

"Let's see. We have a pair of handcuffs, a room all to ourselves, some privacy. I don't know. What do you think we should do?"

He'd taken the right tack. Her tension eased and she managed a smile. "I think we should talk."

He grinned. "Now why doesn't that surprise me? Come on. Let's sit down. We might as well make ourselves comfortable while we wait." He helped her onto the one small bed the cell boasted and tucked her close. "So what do you want to talk about?"

"Diana Starr."

That didn't take long. He sighed. "What do you want to know about her?"

"First...what did you whisper in her ear before she left?"

"I promised to invite her to our wedding."

"Oh, very funny. What did you really say?"

"If you're going to question every answer I give, I'm gonna catch some shut-eye. Now do you want to argue or do you want to talk?"

"Talk." About Diana, no doubt. Sure enough, she started in again. "She kept calling you lover. Is she really your lover? Or rather, was she?"

"Nope. She calls everybody that. Including her husband."

"She's *married*?"

"Has been ever since we first met. And quite happily, too."

"Then why did she come here?"

"She told you that. She came to try to talk me out of ending our partnership."

"I assume she wasn't successful?"

"Not even a little."

"So she's left and won't ever be back as long as she lives?"

"Don't sound so hopeful." He tortured her for a full two minutes before putting her out of her misery. "Diana won't be back any time soon."

There was a slight pause, then, "I thought her hairstyle was rather interesting. Didn't you?"

"Forget it, sweetheart. I like your hair just how it is."

"I don't recall asking your opinion." She wrinkled her nose in contemplation. "Purple spikes would give people something to talk about, don't you think?"

"Are you asking my opinion now?"

"Yes."

"Don't even think about it."

"Okay." She was silent for far too long, which didn't bode well for him. Sure enough, she murmured, "There's something else I think we need to discuss."

"What's that?" he asked warily.

"My...seduction."

"Getting impatient?"

"No." She glanced at him, her expression surprisingly serious. "You need to stop for a while, Sam."

He hadn't expected that. He'd thought her enthusiasm for her downfall matched his own. Apparently, that had changed since this morning. "Diana is not my lover," he stated in an even voice.

"This isn't about Diana."

"Then what is it about?"

"You've only been back two short days and I..." She took a deep breath. "I can't seem to control myself around you."

He struggled to hide his amusement. "I'm happy to hear it."

She tucked a windswept lock of hair behind her ear. "I'm not." She drew her knees up to her chest and wrapped her arms around her legs, dragging his arm along for the ride. "I need time to get my bearings, to decide if I want to be—"

"A fallen woman?"

She studied him with bleak eyes. "I almost was today," she whispered. "You take my breath away, Sam. You steal every thought from my head."

"You're not the only one, Annie. You do one hell of a number on me, as well." Her mouth trembled and he struggled to harden himself to its appeal. "I'm not letting you go."

"I'm only asking for some time," she pleaded.

"You've had seven years."

"And now I'm asking for some more."

He tilted his head against the wall behind him and fought for control. "How much longer?"

"I don't know."

He clenched his teeth to keep from arguing, to keep from ending her doubts by taking what he wanted. It would be easy, so incredibly easy. One kiss and she'd be his. "Fine. I'll give you a few days. As soon as we get back to Myrtle's, I'll move over to Soundings."

"Sam, I'm—"

"What the *hell* were you thinkin', boy?" Rolly's voice thundered down the hallway, the intrusion as unwelcome as it was untimely. "You locked Annie and Sam up together?"

"There was only one cell, Sheriff," they could hear Bertie protesting. "But I kept them handcuffed. There's not much trouble they can get up to with handcuffs on."

"Have you lost your ever-lovin' mind? It's probably a fantasy come true for the boy. An innocent girl, a pair of handcuffs, a jail cell. Good heavenly days, son. You're married, aren't you? Use your imagination." Rolly appeared in the doorway, eyeing them suspiciously.

"We haven't done anything," Annie announced, leaping to her feet. "Just in case you were wondering."

"I'm relieved to hear it." He released a gusty sigh. "I'm sorry about this, Miss Annie. Bertie overstepped himself this time."

"It was my fault, Sheriff Rawling. I was speeding and riding without a helmet *and* driving without my license on me."

"Yes, well, you should know better than that," he scolded. "Especially the helmet."

"You're right. It won't happen again."

"In that case, I'll let you go with a warning." Rolly glanced at Bertie and jerked his head toward the cell. "Open up, boy. And get those handcuffs off them."

"Yes, sir, Sheriff."

"What's Beaumont in here for?"

"He was with her."

"Did he do anything wrong?" Hope blossomed in the sheriff's voice.

"Nothing worth jailing him for," Bertie hastened to assure.

Rolly didn't bother to hide his disappointment. "Guess you can let him go, too."

"Thanks, Sheriff," Sam thought to say.

"Don't go thankin' me, Beaumont." Rolly offered a sharklike grin. "I have every expectation of havin' you back in here real soon."

Sam returned the grin. "If Annie's part of the deal, you won't have to bother with an invite. I'll hurry right over."

To Annie's utter disappointment, Sam did just as he said. The minute they returned to Myrtle's, he packed his bags and moved into Soundings. Supposedly, he was working on repairs to his house. Not that she knew for certain since she didn't have the nerve to see for herself. But everyone she ran into took great delight in detailing his every movement.

It wasn't until after dinner of their sixth day apart that she even saw him and then it was only because Pansy lost her temper and insisted Annie go "put the poor man out of his misery." Fortunately, she managed to come up with an acceptable reason to explain her visit, one she silently rehearsed as she trailed him to his boathouse.

"Hey there," she greeted, dithering in the doorway and looking around. The structure appeared unexpectedly sturdy, considering it hadn't received any attention in the past seven years. The rough plank walls were all in place, as was the tin roof.

"Hey there yourself," he said, looking up from the box he was investigating. "This is a surprise."

"For me, too. In all honesty, I hadn't planned to come over."

His grin flashed in the fading light. "Then why have you?"

She shrugged sheepishly, stepping into the shack. "Pansy made me," she confessed. "And I also wanted to see if you needed help. They're saying on the weather channel that we could get a piece of that hurricane heading up the coast now that it's decided to leave Florida alone. So..." She offered a bright smile. "Need any help?"

"That's one of the reasons I'm out here. I'm checking to see if everything's secured. Although I doubt we'll be hit. They say it's going inland well south of us."

"That's what I'm hoping, too." She glanced around, looking for an excuse to linger. "I didn't realize you actually had a boat in here." It rested on supports, its wooden hull clear of the dirt floor. "Is it seaworthy?"

"It will be, when I get around to the repairs."

"Will you take me out in it?"

"Count on it."

Behind her, the door creaked closed, startling her. Odd. There wasn't much of a breeze tonight. "Well, I guess I should be going. It's getting late and..." He started for her and she froze, dragging in a quick breath.

"And Myrtle will worry." He brushed past. "Let me get the door."

"Sam, wait." She gritted her teeth and said the words she should have offered seven long years ago. "I wanted to apologize."

He hesitated, his hand on the latch. "What for?"

"For hurting you. I should never have sent the Musketeers after you." She twisted her hands together. "I know you said you were going to seduce me to get even, but it's not necessary anymore. You know that, don't you?"

"Come again?"

"You don't have to keep up the seduction routine," she persisted doggedly. "Everyone gets the point. You had every right to try to even the score. And now that you've had some fun at my expense, you can end the game."

He tilted his head to one side, his eyes unreadable in the gloom. "What if I don't want to end it?"

"Don't you see?" she said earnestly. "If you keep it up, it could get serious. People think it's funny now. But if it goes much further, that will change. They might turn on you, Sam. And I couldn't bear for that to happen."

"Believe it or not, Annie, I know precisely what I'm doing."

"Then you're still going to ruin me?"

He leaned down, his lips inches from hers. "A promise is a promise." He turned back to the door and tugged at the latch...and tugged some more. "Dammit! Not again."

"What's wrong?"

His mouth compressed in a tight line. "You're not going to believe this, sweetheart. But the door's locked."

CHAPTER SEVEN

ANNIE stared in disbelief. "It's what?"

Sam shrugged. "You heard me. Locked. Bolted. Barred. Or barricaded. Take your pick."

"You know, this is getting downright ridiculous." She planted her hands on her hips. "I've lived on this island for twenty-five years and I've had more freak accidents happen the past couple of weeks than in all those years combined." She looked at him sharply. "Makes you wonder, doesn't it?"

His expression of innocence would have done an angel proud—a fallen angel, that was. "You think it's my fault?"

"Did you lock us in here?" she demanded point-blank.
"No."

Absolute. Unequivocal. And totally believable. "Then how did it happen?"

"That's an interesting question. One I'd even give some of my IBM stock to have explained."

Now she really was convinced of his innocence. "You must have some idea."

"Oh, I've got plenty of ideas. Just no proof."

She glared at the door. It was growing late, and unless the Three Musketeers got wind of their predicament soon, rescue before dawn was fast becoming an unlikely event. "How long do you think we'll be stuck in here?" she asked, hoping Sam would give her the reassurance she sought.

He shrugged. "Until somebody decides to come by and unlock the door."

"I know that!"

He made himself comfortable on a pile of burlap bags. "Then why ask?"

She didn't answer but strode to the door again and shook the latch. "If I weren't a lady, I'd pound on the door and scream my fool head off. Aw, shoot." She balled her fists and banged as long and hard as she could. "*Let me out of here!*"

"Give it up, Annie. You're only going to hurt—"

"Goldang it!" She cradled her hand.

"—yourself. You did, didn't you?"

She peered at the meaty part of her palm and winced. She'd scraped it up good. "I think I got another splinter. Or maybe this one's left over from when I climbed down the oak tree."

"Fell out of said tree."

"Whatever."

He held out his hand. "Here. Let me see."

"I can take care of it."

"Like you've taken care of all our other predicaments?"

She lifted her chin. "That's right."

He released his breath in an impatient sigh. "Stop being so damned stubborn and get over here, Annie. Let me see what you've done to yourself."

"Sam Beaumont, you are the bossiest man I've ever had the misfortune to cross paths with. It's just a splinter and I can darn well take care of it myself."

He didn't bother arguing. Crossing to her side, he seized her hand and held it within a shaft of fast-fading sunshine. It arrowed through a knothole in the plank wall and landed on her palm like a sprinkle of gold dust. Sam examined her wound, light gilding the side of his face, as well, before being swallowed by the fierce darkness of his hair.

"Face facts, sweetheart," he said pragmatically. "As much as it pains me to admit it, you couldn't take care of a mouse in a field full of ripe corn."

That just had to be an insult, if she could only figure out why. "What's that supposed to mean?"

"Hang on." He squeezed the ball of her palm uncomfortably tight for an instant. "Got it. Better?"

"Yes, thanks." She sucked on the wound. "Come on, Sam. Explain what's earned me your latest insult. What haven't I caught on to yet that you have?"

"We're being set up."

"Set up?" she repeated, staring at him blankly. "You mean someone locked us in here *on purpose*?"

"You're kidding, right? They locked us in here, syphoned off the gas in your outboard engine, sabotaged my doorknobs after I'd repaired them and locked us up in jail while still handcuffed together. And none of that struck you as the least bit odd?"

"Well, I've noticed we keep getting stuck in the strangest situations. But I thought—"

"What? That they were accidents? Coincidences?"

"I guess I don't have as suspicious a mind as you do." She regarded him curiously. "What makes you believe it's deliberate?"

"Think about it, Annie. Someone had to barricade the door. It didn't do that all on its lonesome."

She stirred uneasily. "I figured it locked automatically whenever the door closed."

"Nope. It wasn't locked when I first opened it. Only when we tried to get out. I'm guessing somebody gave that door a helping hand."

His wry tone brought a reluctant smile to her face. "But...who?"

"Like I said, I have my suspicions."

She perched on the edge of a barrel, fixing him with an avid gaze. "So? Come on, spill it."

"I'm guessing it's the same person who beat the tar out of me seven years ago. You remember. The night the Three Musketeers threw me off the island."

She slowly stood. "*What*?"

"Oh, did I neglect to mention that minor detail?" he asked with mock innocence.

"Yes, you neglected to mention it!" She couldn't contain her shock. "Dear heaven, Sam. Are you serious? Someone beat you up that night?"

"You didn't know?"

"*No!*" An image blossomed in her mind—fists impacting on flesh, Sam's flesh. Sam, battered and bruised and barely conscious, left without a backward glance. Sam, without the strength to get help, alone and hurt, no doubt cursing the one responsible for his pain. Tears burned her eyes. Cursing *her* since she was the one responsible. Her lungs closed up as though seized in an iron fist. "Sam!" She fought for air. "I...I can't breathe. I can't..."

He was beside her in an instant, holding her close. "Easy does it, sweetheart. It was a long time ago. I'm fine. None the worse for wear, in case you hadn't noticed."

His reassurance didn't help. The tears came anyway, noisy, inelegant, gut-wrenching sobs, escaping in a uncontrollable torrent. She'd never been one to cry pretty. "They hurt you. Why did they do that?"

"It's what men do when they're angry and helpless. They strike out."

"But I told them it was my fault. I told them you hadn't done anything wrong." She fumbled in the pocket of her dress and pulled out a tissue. It fluttered helplessly in her hand like a wounded bird. "I told them I'd changed my mind but didn't have the nerve to face you."

"Apparently, they put their own spin on things."

"What happened?" she demanded the instant her tears had abated enough for her to think straight. Anger slowly took hold, helping to swamp all other emotions. "Who attacked you?"

"Someone jumped me after I was dumped at the ferry dock."

"*Who?*"

"I never saw him. It was dark and he caught me from behind while I was working to get free of the ropes."

"And he hit you?"

"Gave me a right good pounding. Since I was still tied up, it was a little difficult to return the favor."

"Oh, Sam!" The air shuddered through her lungs. "I'm so sorry. I never meant—"

"It was a long time ago," he soothed. "And I'm fairly certain you were just the excuse for the attack. The fury coming off whoever it was felt personal."

She applied the tissue to her eyes and nose. "You suspect either Ben or the mayor or the sheriff, though, don't you?" It made her heartsick to level the accusation. She hated to think it could be any of them. But then, she hated to think anyone on the island would be capable of such violence.

"They're the most logical choices. For the record, when I returned to the island and confronted them, they denied it."

"Did you believe them?"

He started to answer but hesitated. "I thought so."

"Something's happened to change your mind." It wasn't a question.

"When I met with them, I warned they weren't to interfere this time around."

"Interfere how?"

His grin said it all. Interfere in his seduction of her.

It was hard to maintain one's dignity while turning six shades of red. Fortunately, the light was dim enough she hoped he wouldn't notice. His teasing also helped dry the last of her tears. "I can't believe you told them that."

"Actually, I didn't. What I said was that I'd come back for you and they weren't to get in my way."

"And from that they assumed you meant..." She cleared her throat. "You know."

"Since my less-than-noble intentions were all over the island within the hour, I suspect that was precisely what they assumed."

She nibbled on her lip as she sorted through all he'd told her. "I don't understand something. You told them to back off...but they haven't. Every time we've been—"

"Compromised?"

"*Almost* compromised, they've rescued me."

His eyebrows shot upward. "Hell, sweetheart. I didn't realize you needed rescuing from me."

"You know what I mean."

"It means I haven't been doing a very good job seducing you if you consider their bad timing a rescue."

"You're ignoring the point."

"How crass of me."

"Sam! The point is...they *have* been rescuing me. Your warning didn't work."

"Actually, it was more of a threat than a warning," he confessed with a charming smile.

"You *threatened* them?"

He shrugged. "I wanted to make sure they stayed out of my business this time."

"You mean—" her chin betrayed her by quivering "—you threatened them and they still rescued me?"

"Yeah." He shook his head in disgust. "Who'd have figured they'd be so damned noble."

"What did you threaten them with?"

"Oh, not much. Public disgrace, revealing a few secrets they'd rather keep hidden. The usual dastardly deeds."

"I can't believe you did that!"

For a brief instant, his expression hardened. "I was determined to get what I wanted."

"Me. Or rather, your revenge on me." She pulled free of his arms. "But those three dear, sweet men wouldn't let you."

"Let's not get carried away. Two are dear, sweet men. One of them's the SOB who attacked me and is now sneaking around doing everything he can think of to assist in your downfall." Sam chuckled. "It must be aggravating him something fierce that the other two keep getting wind of his antics and riding to your rescue. Not to mention dragging him along, too, forcing him to undo all his hard work."

"Oh." She perched on the edge of the barrel again. "So, which one of them is it?"

"I can't quite figure that out. Odds are it's Rolly."

"Why the sheriff?"

"Because he has a mean right hook." Sam rubbed his jaw. "Whoever pounded on me that night knew what he was doing. I can't see Ben or the mayor having the skill or nerve to pull off a stunt like that, can you?"

"To be honest, I can't see Sheriff Rawling doing it,

either. He might be a mite hotheaded. But he's not mean."

"I'll have to take your word for it. Not that it matters."

She was almost afraid to ask. "Why doesn't it matter?"

"Whoever it is hopes to get back in my good graces. He figures helping to compromise you will do it, and all will be forgiven."

"And will it?"

"No." There was just enough light left to see the ruthlessness blacken his eyes. "When I find out who jumped me that night, he'll be next on my list to take care of."

She shivered at his tone. It was so hard and cold and final. Apparently, forgiveness wasn't a virtue Sam intended to cultivate—which didn't bode well for her. If Sam's attacker was next on his list, that meant she occupied the top spot. Assuming no one arrived in time tonight—a very real possibility—he'd undoubtedly attain his goal.

And then what?

"What happens after I'm ruined?" she asked nervously.

"Haven't you figured that out yet?"

"Not really." She crossed to the door and tugged at it. Nothing had changed since she'd last tried, but a girl could always hope. Slowly, she turned, pressing her back against the rough wood. "Maybe no one will believe anything happened."

"Maybe."

She edged toward the barrel, not that it offered any more protection than the door. "Unlikely is what you really mean."

Sam picked up an armful of the burlap sacks he'd been sitting on and dumped them into the boat. "Highly unlikely. I haven't made any secret of my intentions. If we're trapped here overnight, everyone will assume the worst." His grin flashed in the darkness. "Or the best."

"And then you'll go on your merry way? Return to New York?"

"Nope. I plan to make my home here, remember?"

For some reason, she found the reminder reassuring. "Oh, right. Plus you still have more people to destroy. I'm just at the top of the list." She wished it wasn't quite so dark so she could determine whether his expression remained as merciless as before, or whether that odd tenderness that she glimpsed every so often tempered his rancor.

Another armful of sacks went into the boat. "You sound worried."

"I am." She deserted the barrel to slip toward the side of the boat farthest from him. "Sam?"

"Yes, sweetheart?"

"I'm not sure I want to be ruined. I don't think I'll like it as much as I thought."

"Don't you trust me?"

She probably should think about her answer some, but her brain apparently had better things to do. "I've always trusted you. I always will."

"Then trust me when I say that you'll like it just fine." He shook out a thick quilted pad and spread it over the sacks lining the bottom of the boat.

"What about the man who attacked you?"

"I'm afraid he's not going to enjoy his ruination nearly as much as you'll enjoy yours."

She couldn't think of a single blessed thing to say to that, so she chose silence. Outside, she could hear the gentle splash of the water as it lapped against the marsh grass outside the boathouse. Locusts sawed away in the trees nearby and bullfrogs bellowed so loudly it was a wonder they ever attracted a mate. Who would want to put up with such a noisy fellow? In the distance, a screech owl called, the eerie sound a cross between a whinny and a groan.

The awkward silence finally spurred her into speech. "Owls should hoot, not make ghost noises," she announced.

"Come here, Annie."

"Okay." She twisted her hands together, surprised to discover her legs were trembling. "But you realize I'm honor bound to fight you."

"You won't fight. Come on." He held out his hand. "No point in delaying the inevitable."

She forced her feet to move, reluctantly circling the boat toward him. "I thought you didn't want to have premarital sex with me. I thought you weren't going to have any babies out of wedlock because of all the taunts you suffered as a child. Because of your mother, I mean." She drew to a halt just beyond his reach.

"We don't need to worry about that. You won't conceive my child tonight." Was that laughter she heard in his voice. What could he possibly find amusing at a time like this? "I promise. I'll take care of everything."

"Everything." It took a moment for the significance of his comment to sink in. "You came prepared? You expected us to get into another predicament?" she demanded, outraged. "I can't believe it! How could you?"

He was definitely laughing now. "The way things were going, I thought one of us better."

She planted her hands on her hips. "What do you mean by that crack? How what was going?"

"Your seduction. We've been progressing quite well, in case you hadn't noticed."

"I hadn't!" She worked a bit on her temper, quite relieved when it heated right up. "I think you have a lot of nerve coming out to the boathouse with your pockets stuffed with…with—"

"Hope?"

"Naughty intentions," she snapped.

"The important thing is that my naughty intentions, as you so delicately put it, will be well covered. Now, shut up, Annie, and get over here."

Not a chance. "That's disgraceful. It truly is," she informed him. "Have you no shame?"

"None."

"What will Aunt Myrtle say?"

"About damned time."

"She most certainly would not," Annie groused. "Myrtle doesn't swear."

"Yes, she does swear. But only when provoked something fierce. My guess is our situation has done just that."

"Only because Aunt Myrtle doesn't have a clue what you've been up to." He scooped her up into his arms, taking her by surprise. "Don't!" she shrieked, burying her face against his shoulder. When he didn't immediately do anything, she peeked up at him. "Sam?"

He released a long-suffering sigh. "Yes, sweetheart?"

"Are you really going to ruin me?"

"I'm afraid so."

"Okay. But be gentle. I haven't done this before."

"So your sign says." For a man intent on revenge, there was a wealth of tenderness lacing his voice. "If it makes you feel any better, I've never seduced a virgin before."

"Oh, well," she said a tad breathlessly, "you know what they say. Practice makes perfect."

Laughter rumbled through his chest. "I suspect this will be a one-shot deal."

"That's a relief," she chattered nervously. "I don't think the islanders will tolerate an ongoing process of..." She waved a hand in the air. "You know."

He swung her over the gunwale of the boat and set her carefully on top of the pad covering the burlap sacks. "I don't expect they'll tolerate this one, either."

She scooted to one side. "Then why do it? You don't have to." He'd have had to be deaf to miss the beseeching note in her voice.

"I'm afraid the choice is out of our hands." In one easy move, he vaulted into the boat and settled beside her. He lay back, urging her down, as well, cushioning her head on his shoulder. "It's not the most comfortable bed in the world, but I've had worse."

"Really?" She played with the top button of his shirt. "When?"

"Before I lived with Myrtle. Lots of nights, my parents would fight and I'd slip outside to escape the shouting. Sleeping under the stars was quieter, but the mosquitoes made it a tad uncomfortable."

"I didn't realize." He'd rarely mentioned his parents when they dated. In fact, he'd been quite deft at changing the subject the few times it arose. "I know your mother died when you were ten," she prompted tentatively. "What happened to your father?"

"He took off."

"Have you ever gone looking for him?"

"Nope. And he's never come looking for me. Seems like a fair trade-off to me."

"Oh."

"Relax, Annie. Nothing's going to happen that you don't want to have happen."

She cleared her throat. "What, exactly, are you planning to do?"

"I thought I might kiss you for a while."

Kissing. She wouldn't mind that so much. She rather liked kissing Sam. But kissing tended to lead to other things. "And then what?"

"Well, then I thought I might unbutton the front of your dress."

She swallowed. "It...it is a bit stuffy in here. Fortunately, I wore more undergarments than usual, so it won't be totally improper. Sort of like wearing a bathing suit."

"Now I'm curious." He plucked at the clasp anchoring her hair on top of her head. "What is your...bathing suit made out of?"

She shrugged, feeling the slow slide of curls tumble toward her shoulders. "The usual."

"Lace?" The clasp pinged against the far wall as he tossed it aside.

"I believe it has some lace, yes."

"And silk?"

She gave a ladylike snort. "Sorry to disappoint you. I'm a cotton sort of girl."

"I've always liked that about you." He twined a lock of hair around his finger. "A lace-and-cotton bathing suit, huh?"

"Well...the top half of it is. The rest is just plain ol' cotton." She was starting to tremble and knew he felt it. She rushed into speech again. "Cotton is surprisingly sturdy. It doesn't rip very easily."

"I wasn't planning on ripping anything," he reassured her. "Just unbuttoning."

"Oh." A silence stretched between them, growing more and more unbearable. Unable to stand it another minute, she blurted, "After you unbutton, what were you thinking might happen?"

He chuckled, the sound a low rumble. "Why then I'd have to check out your bathing suit. See what parts are lace and what parts are cotton. Since it's so dark, I might have to feel my way around. If I still couldn't get a good sense of what's what, I'd be forced to slip that bathing suit clean off you."

Oh, dear heaven! "I don't think that's such a good idea."

"No?"

She shook her head, her heart pounding wildly. "Absolutely not."

"In that case, I guess I'd be reduced to pulling a few things down. Or if I'm feeling real ambitious, pushing a few things up. Whatever it takes to get them out of the way. I'll probably even toss any excess overboard. Like your hair holder."

"It's called a clasp." Her breathing grew constricted. "I'd rather you didn't do that. The throwing-over part, I mean. I'd pretty much like everything to stay right where it is."

"Ah, but that would defeat the purpose."

It wasn't difficult to read between the lines. It would be tough to make love to a girl with her clothes on. "What if...what if I tried to stop you? What if I got nervous?" Or scared.

"Are you nervous when I kiss you?"

"No," she confessed. Nor was she scared.

His lips caressed her temple, exciting a shiver. "Were you nervous last time I unbuttoned your dress?"

"Not really." Not until the Three Musketeers showed up. And even then, she'd been more embarrassed than nervous.

"You won't be nervous this time, either."

"But unbuttoning...that's all you're going to do?"

"Well...not quite." He waited a beat before adding, "I believe I mentioned that I'm a tactile sort. I like to feel my way through a predicament."

"You're going to touch me, aren't you?"

"For certain."

He rolled onto his side, facing her, and she braced herself for impact. When it didn't come, she relaxed minutely. "I don't think that's such a good idea."

"If it would make you more comfortable, once I'm done examining that bathing suit of yours, I'll start at your feet and work my way up."

Feet. That was good. Feet were a good distance from other, more intimate spots. "I'd probably need you to give them lots of attention."

"I wouldn't want all the other parts to miss out on the action."

"No problem. My feet work harder than any other part. They deserve only the best."

"Fair enough. Once I'm finished there—"

"It'll be morning."

She sensed his grin. "Not quite. We'll still have a couple of hours to spare. Plenty of time for the rest of what I have in mind."

"Rest?"

"Like your calves. Of course, calves lead right up to knees. And once you're at the knees, it's just a short slide to your thighs." He paused, allowing her imagination to run riot. "After that, we'll take a minute for some of that pushing up and pulling down."

Her skirt and her underpants. Warmth pooled deep in her loins. "Please, Sam. You have to stop."

"You won't stop me, Annie." His mouth was inches

from her ear, his words whisper soft. "Because it'll be what you want, too. You'll want me to touch you, want to feel my hands on you, stroking you where no one has before. Clothes will be a barrier, a barrier you'll be only too happy to be rid of."

"No." Was that heavy, velvety voice hers…a voice that vibrated with passionate longing? "I can't."

"You will. When I touch you, you'll open to me. Offer yourself to me. Weep for me. Sheathe me. And I'll complete you. Love you. Take you to a place that's uniquely ours."

"Why, Sam? Why me?"

"Because you're ready, Annie. It's your time."

"And tomorrow?"

"With any luck at all, when tomorrow comes, we'll do it all again. Do you trust me?"

She shouldn't. Nevertheless, she did. "I trust you." She hesitated before admitting, "I won't stop you. Somehow I suspect you already knew that, didn't you?"

"Yes. But you needed to know it, too. Now, close your eyes." The minute she had, he spooned her against him. His arms were wrapped tightly around her, his chest warming her back, his shoulder still pillowing her head. "Sleep now, sweetheart. There'll be plenty of time to ruin you in the morning."

"Do you promise?"

"You'll see. By morning, there won't be any question that you're mine."

CHAPTER EIGHT

THE wind had picked up by morning, the air balmy and thick with the scent of rain. It whipped through the cracks in the wall and moved the dust in miniature whirlwinds. Sam stirred and sat up.

"What are you doing?" Annie asked drowsily.

"Taking off my shirt."

He settled down beside her again, rolling her onto her back and pulling her close. "It's time, sweetheart."

She yawned, struggling to separate sweet dreams from an even sweeter reality. "Time for what?"

"For this."

He lowered himself gently on top of her. The instant full awareness dawned, her lips parted eagerly, welcoming his possession. His mouth found hers, hard where she was soft, skilled where she still had a lot of catching up to do. She felt him fumbling with the front of her dress, one hand slipping buttons through holes, while the other cupped her breast through the white cotton dress.

"I just remembered. You promised you wouldn't do that anymore," she managed to say. "When we were on the sandbar, remember? You said you'd wait a week."

"I lied." He peeled back the edges of her dress, finding the scrap of lace and cotton beneath, just as she'd described. "Though it wasn't much of a lie since our week'll be up in a few hours. Besides, last night I told you I planned to do precisely this." He trailed a finger along the edge of her "bathing suit" top. "And more. I don't recall your complaining then."

"It must have escaped my mind." Her eyes fluttered shut as though by not looking, nothing untoward could happen. "Just out of curiosity…why didn't you do anything last night?"

"I had an excellent reason at the time."

"Which was?"

"Damned if I can recall."

His hand drifted to her legs and he inched the skirt of her dress toward her knees. The air escaped her lungs in a heated rush. "Maybe we shouldn't do this," she protested nervously. "Somebody might come."

"I know. Relax, love. It'll be over soon."

"Over soon? Wait a minute! What happened to pulling up and pushing down? What happened to leg massages? And going to places no one has gone to before? If you think you can just toss my dress over my head and—"

He dammed the flood of words with his mouth, his kiss a tender, almost apologetic caress, filled with frightening finality. "I'm sorry, Annie. It's out of my hands now."

"What do you mean? I don't understand." That's when she heard it. Heard the angry voices and the stomp of feet. "Oh, no!" She struggled to free herself from his arms, to escape the nest he'd made in the bottom of the dry-docked boat.

"Annie, stop it! You're going to tip us—"

With a loud groan of aging timbers, the boat shifted. Annie shrieked as she tumbled sideways, instantly buried beneath dusty burlap and one large male body. Sam was shaking, she realized a confused second later. And then it hit her. He was laughing. Before she could do more than give his shoulder a good pummeling, the door to the boathouse crashed inward.

"Annie! Annie, are you all right?"

"I'm fine, Bertie. But could you—"

"She's here!" the deputy shouted to those behind him. "And so's Sam. He's finally done it, boys. He's compromised Annie. Get the preacher. There's gonna be a wedding!"

"No! No! Nothing happened, I swear. All we did was talk about what we'd do. We didn't actually…" She fought to free herself of burlap, dust and Sam's wandering hands. "Stop that," she ordered in a furious whisper. "You're doing it on purpose. They're going to think we've been up to something if you don't cut it out."

"We have been up to something."

"But not *that*."

"We could have been."

"Just let me—"

Abruptly, Sam's weight lifted from her and she heard a soft thud, followed by a softer grunt. She scrambled to her feet and ran out of the boathouse, momentarily blinded by the sun. She blinked rapidly, realizing that Sam had disappeared into a ring of men. It didn't take a lot of thought to figure out what they were doing to him.

She ripped into the center of the circle. "Leave him alone. He hasn't done anything."

Bertie, who was busily pulling a pile of men off Sam, gaped at her, then turned a bright shade of red. "Annie, you might want to…" He gestured to the front of her dress.

She looked down and gasped, yanking the halves of her dress together. Not that it was much better closed. A dusty handprint marred the virginal white bodice. "I swear, nothing happened."

Sam released a pained laugh and struggled to his feet. "You're never going to convince them of that," he said, brushing off his clothes. "Not looking like you do. And not after spending a night in the boathouse with me."

She knew how it must appear. Her hair slid down her back in a hopeless tangle, the brisk wind adding to its unruly state. Her lips felt swollen from this morning's kisses, and no doubt looked it, too. Her dress was wrinkled and smudged. She glanced downward. And it gaped as widely as the mouths of the people surrounding them.

Reverend Pulcher arrived just then. "Oh, Annie," he said with a disappointed sigh. "Now you'll have to take down your sign."

"You can marry them, though, can't you, Reverend?" Bertie asked anxiously. "Today?"

"That isn't necessary," Annie insisted.

Six shotguns lifted to level on Sam. "I believe it is," he contradicted ever so gently. "I suspect it's either that or a funeral. I'm pulling for a wedding if you don't have any serious objections."

"But nothing happened!"

Rolly regarded her with a skeptical frown. "Do you mean to tell me you two didn't do anything but sit and talk all night?"

"We slept," Annie replied.

"And kissed," Sam offered helpfully.

"But that's all!"

"Well...not quite." The Beaumont smile was back in place as cocky as ever. "But being a gentleman, I don't think it's appropriate to go into details."

"Oh! This is ridiculous."

Mayor Pike shook his head. "Give it up, girl. We let you off the hook last time. But that dress of yours is all the proof we need that there were monkeyshines going on last night. If this were a courtroom, you'd be tried, convicted and hanged on that bit of evidence alone. Ben, go round up my clerk,'' he instructed. ''I'll need to get their license taken care of so the preacher here can marry them.''

''I'm not marrying anyone!'' Not that they listened. Bertie dragged her off to one side.

''Button up your dress, Annie. This is all for the best and you know it. You've been wanting to marry Sam Beaumont since you were four years old. And think of all the good it'll do the town. Now that he's ruined you, he doesn't have to ruin anyone else.'' He reached into his pocket and pulled out a comb. ''Like to fix your hair?''

She worked at the buttons of her dress. ''No, I wouldn't like to fix my hair.''

''To be honest, Annie, it's a bit of a mess. I think you want to.''

She swatted his hand away. ''Why is it that everyone's so darned busy telling me what I should and shouldn't do?''

Bertie shrugged. ''You've been doing it all these years. I guess it's our turn now.''

''I want to go home. Come on, Bertie,'' she wheedled. ''Be a pal. Get me out of this.''

''I'm afraid that'll have to wait until after the ceremony.''

''You don't understand. I want to go *now*.'' She gave him her fiercest frown. But for the first time in all the years she'd known him, it didn't work.

''I'm sorry, Annie. Rolly said that if the worst had happened, I was to escort you to the church personally. And that's what I aim to do.''

''You're not going to let me change first?'' she asked, outraged.

"You look just fine." As a lie, it was a pretty pathetic one and they both knew it.

She sighed. "All right. I'll go to the church with you. But that doesn't mean I'm going to marry anyone."

"I don't see that you have much choice." He slanted her an apologetic look. "Being a Delacorte and all, folks will expect you to do the proper thing. Especially you, Annie."

And that said it all. The purple hair, the motorcycle and dresses, the belly scar, that darned sign… None of it mattered. To the islanders, she was still a Delacorte and that meant death before dishonor. Of course, she could always stand up and tell them the truth. Tell them why it didn't matter. But that option wasn't available to her. Her only choice was to refuse to marry Sam. And when she did that, she'd end up humiliating him in public all over again.

Unfortunately, she didn't have any choice.

To Annie's silent fury, she wasn't given time to refuse anything. A marriage application was brought into the tiny room where she'd been ensconced. Someone had already filled in the pertinent details—Pansy, if the handwriting was anything to go by. All that remained for her to do was sign the document. With Rolly, Ben and Mayor Pike standing over her, scowling like a trio of outraged fathers, she found herself hastily scrawling her signature on the appropriate line. The mayor handed the document to his clerk and ordered her to notarize, witness, stamp and "clerkify" whatever else was necessary to make it legal. Then the group bustled back out, leaving her alone to contemplate the error of her ways.

Of course, the only error she could come up with was not having enjoyed the transgression she'd been accused of. Maybe it would have been some small compensation if she'd had the pleasure in addition to the punishment.

Five minutes later, Pansy appeared in the doorway, looking rather windblown. "Phew! It sure is blowing out there. I wonder if we're going to get a piece of that hurricane after all." Noting Annie's expression, she offered a sympathetic smile. "It's time, sweetie."

Annie folded her arms across her chest. "I'm not doing it."

"Sure you are. Bertie said so." As if that ended the discussion, she bellied her way in and handed Annie a large, square box as well as a small bouquet of flowers tied with a sunny yellow ribbon. "The veil I wore when I got married is in the box," Pansy explained. "Myrtle added some fresh flowers so it would look pretty."

"That was fast work."

"Yes, well...we figured it was only a matter of time before Sam managed to compromise you and you had to get married. So we had everything lined up."

Annie stared at her sister in disbelief. "You've been expecting this?"

"Of course! Goodness, haven't you heard? They have a pool goin' down at Drake's. Everyone's taking bets on the day and hour Sam would be marched up the aisle with the business end of a shotgun at his back. Listen, if you'd delay the ceremony just another half hour, I'd really appreciate it. The hens bet on nine-thirty today. But I've got ten dollars riding on ten o'clock."

"I don't believe it!"

"You better. I never joke about money." Pansy opened the box and removed the garland and veil. She set it on Annie's head, then frowned. "It might look better once you've had a good brushing. And darn it all, I

didn't think to bring you a change of clothes. I swear, I
don't know where my head is these days."

"I don't want a brush or a change of clothes. Pansy,
I want to go home."

"I guess you should have thought about that before
you and Sam did it in the boathouse for the world to
see."

It took all Annie's willpower to keep from screaming.
"We didn't *do* it. We just talked about it."

"A waste of words, if you ask me." Pansy grinned.
"And here I always thought Sam was a man of action.
How disappointing."

He is, Annie almost said before thinking better of it.
"Sam will put a stop to this."

"I really don't think so."

"Why not? He can't want to marry me. He was after
revenge, not matrimony."

"Now that's something you'll have to take up with
him. But I suspect he's not going to do much arguing
with all those shotguns aimed his way." Pansy gave her
a final once-over, then nodded. "Well, you're not the
cleanest bride I've ever seen, but you surely are the prettiest."

"Pansy—"

"Not another word. Now give me a hug and kiss and
go get your man. He's waited a long time for this moment."

"You sound like Myrtle."

"Why, thank you, sister dear. That's a sweet thing to
say." Pansy gave her a fierce hug despite her swollen
belly. "I'll tell everyone you're on your way out."

"Everyone?"

"Don't look so surprised. The church is packed. No

one's going to miss the wedding of the town saint." And with that, she disappeared out the door.

For a full minute, Annie considered climbing out a window and hiding until everyone got bored and went home. Then she realized the tiny room didn't boast a window, which meant that she'd have to escape in full view of the entire town. Taking a deep breath, she crossed to the door and yanked it open. It hit the wall with a crash that reverberated throughout the chapel. Pansy hadn't been kidding. The church was jammed with friends and neighbors and relatives. Every last one of them stared at her—not with condemnation as she'd half expected—but with encouraging nods and cheerful smiles. How long would that last?

Reluctantly, she started up the aisle, stumbling to a halt before she'd gone little more than halfway. This was insane. Why was she even here? Just because she'd spent the night in the boathouse with Sam Beaumont did *not* mean she had to marry the man. Every single other individual in this town had done far worse and they hadn't been shoved up the aisle at gunpoint. If that had been the case, Sam's mother wouldn't have been illegitimate.

"Whatcha waiting for, Annie?" Rosie Hinkle called.

"I'm thinking," she shouted.

"Think after the ceremony," Sam replied from his stance near the altar. "Come on up here and let's get this over with."

"Gee, how romantic." She crossed her arms over her chest. "What if I don't want to?"

Releasing a sound of disgust, Sam stalked down the aisle toward her. "Would you rather they blow a hole through me?"

"Maybe."

"Nice." He caught her hand in his and began to tow

her up the aisle. Muffled laughter broke out among the townsfolk. "Come on, Annie. We're getting married and that's all there is to it."

She threw her weight backward and dug in her heels, twisting her veil askew. "I'm not going anywhere," she announced. "Not until I'm good and ready."

He released her so abruptly she stumbled, dropping her bouquet. She landed on her backside, her skirts swirling around her thighs and flowers scattering in a colorful circle around her. She yanked down her dress and glared at her dirty toes. Who'd have thought she, Saint Annie, would end up having a shotgun marriage? Sam reached down and helped her up.

"I don't want to do this," she said quietly. "I don't want to be forced into a marriage that neither of us needs just for the sake of propriety."

"What about for Rolly's sake? And Ben Drake's? And Mayor Pike's? Marrying me will save them, Annie. I'll even agree to end my vendetta. I'll let whichever one of them attacked me off the hook."

"You couldn't hurt them any more than you could me."

A look swept into his face, a look so cold and ruthless it took her breath away. "You don't think so? Try me."

"What will you do if I refuse?" she demanded.

"I think you can guess." He folded his arms across his chest and stared her down. "You'll regret it, I can promise you that much."

He had such a knack for infuriating, for succeeding in getting her to do the exact opposite of what common sense dictated. This time, she wouldn't let him get away with it. This time, she'd be smart. "Then I'll regret it," she announced, turning on her bare little heel.

With an exclamation of disgust, he snagged her around

the waist and tossed her over his shoulder. "If you want to say no, you can say it to Reverend P. But I'm not going to be on the wrong end of a dozen shotguns because of you." He strode down the aisle amid laughter and cheers.

He dumped her on her feet in front of the altar and she fought to gather the remaining shreds of her dignity. "You've gone too far, Beaumont." She tugged at her dress, attempting to shake it into some semblance of order. It was only then that she realized she'd buttoned her bodice crookedly. Giving it up as a lost cause, she swiveled to face the congregation. "You're not really going to allow this to continue, are you?"

"Sure am!" Rosie called out. "You were always the one who said we had a duty to set a good example for the young'uns. After spending the night with Sam Beaumont, marrying him is the only proper thing to do."

She tried one last time. "But we didn't do anything. I'm still the last—well, you know. That 'v' word."

"I beg to differ," Rosie retorted indignantly. "My sweet Alice is a good girl, too."

"Not according to my boy Pete," the mayor snapped back.

A flush mottled Rosie's face. "*What*?" She spun to confront her daughter. "You said the car ran out of gas. You said nothing happened."

"But, Momma, we're in love," Alice wailed. "We were going to tell you just as soon as Pete got a job. We want to get married."

"You march yourself home right this minute, young lady. And Mayor Pike, I expect to see you and Pete at our house this evening to discuss the situation."

"You want to start any more trouble?" Sam asked in an undertone. "Or shall we get this show on the road?"

Tears sparked in her eyes, infuriating her. "There's no reason for us to get married. We didn't do anything."

His gaze smoldered. "We will."

She had to tell him. Now. Before she lost her nerve. "Sam, there's something you need to know first."

"No, there's not."

"You're wrong." She glanced uneasily at Reverend Pulcher. "Could you give us just a moment."

"You had plenty of moments last night, Annie."

"I realize that. And…and I should have mentioned it to Sam when I had the chance." She returned her attention to the man standing rigidly at her side and placed a hand on his arm. "Please. It won't take long."

For an instant, she thought he'd refuse. Then he nodded to the preacher and pulled her off to one side. "Spill it. Quick."

"Pops left a letter before he died."

"So?"

Annie gripped her hands together, fighting to keep from wringing them. "He gave it to his lawyer. And his lawyer's supposed to give it to my fiancé in the event I ever became engaged." She peeked up at him. "We sort of skipped that step, didn't we?" Her attempt at humor failed miserably.

"What's in the letter?"

"I don't know." But she could certainly guess. "When you read it, you won't want to marry me anymore. I expect the lawyer will show up as soon as he hears we got married. And I expect he'll give that letter to you despite your being my husband instead of a measly old fiancé."

"There's nothing your father could say that would keep me from making you my wife."

There was one thing and it had haunted her for seven

long years. "Darn it, Sam," she said in a fierce undertone, "I don't want to marry you only to get divorced the next day."

"There won't be a divorce."

"Sam—"

"Enough, Annie. We're getting married and that's all there is to it."

She dashed tears from her cheeks. "Fine! Just don't say I didn't warn you."

He tipped her chin upward. "You warned me. I understand I'm about to marry a woman with a purple stripe, who rides a motorcycle like some sort of daredevil, who has a belly scar and some horrible, deep dark secret. But I'm that wicked Beaumont boy, remember? I can handle a scandalous wife. In fact, it's expected of me."

"It's not expected of Saint Annie," she whispered miserably. "If you marry me, you'll never be respectable."

"Ah. Curiouser and curiouser. I look forward to reading that letter. I suspect it'll answer a lot of questions."

Her chin trembled no matter how hard she fought to control it. Why didn't she just tell him? She could guess what Pops had said. Maybe if she were the only one whose reputation was at stake, she'd tell the world and to hell with what anyone thought. But she couldn't do that. She was honor bound to keep quiet. "I'm sorry, Sam."

His expression gentled. "For what?"

"For hurting you. I never meant to."

"I realized that a long time ago. It's all right, Annie. Everything will work out. You'll see." He held out his hand. "Ready?"

She didn't argue. What was the point? It wouldn't change a blessed thing. And in the meantime, she'd have a few precious days as his wife. That would make up for all that followed, wouldn't it? After all, Bertie was right. She'd wanted to marry Sam for more years than she could remember. Silently, she slipped her hand into his and walked with him to the altar.

"Everything settled?" Reverend Pulcher asked.

"Yes, sir," Annie murmured.

"You've agreed to marry Sam?"

She nodded, wishing with all her heart that she was dressed in lace and satin instead of coming to Sam a barefoot bride. She wanted to do him proud. Instead, through her own pigheadedness, her hair was a tangle of curls, she wore a smudged dress and no doubt her face was just as dirty, at least the parts that weren't streaked with tears. Oh, yes. Sam had gotten quite a deal.

"And you, Samuel? You're marrying of your own accord?"

He lifted his hands in surrender. "Absolutely, Reverend." A ripple of laughter drifted through the congregation and he lowered his arms, wrapping them around Annie. "Actually, my poor bride's the one who needed convincing. I've been scheming to get her up the aisle ever since I was twelve."

The day he'd crashed her birthday party, she recalled with a start. He'd sauntered in among the hordes of shrieking girls and stopped in front of her. She'd pretended to be furious with him. While all the other girls had hidden under the table or run for the house, she'd leaped to her feet and glared at him, attempting to stare him down. Some part of her, a part far wiser than her years, had sensed he approved of her gumption. He'd laughed, and in that instant, she'd been lost—lost to a pair of wicked black eyes and a grin that could charm the most hardened heart.

He'd helped himself to a piece of the cake right off her plate. And then he'd done the most extraordinary thing. He'd leaned forward and whispered in her ear, "You and me is gettin' married, princess. You see if we don't." Pulling back, he'd gently lifted a lock of her hair and run it through his fingers. She'd never forgotten the look on his face, part curiosity and part amazement, as though he'd discovered something quite exceptional.

Her father had appeared, ripping Sam away from her and knocking him to the ground. She'd darted between the two, giving Sam the opportunity to escape to the beach and the surfboard he'd left there. Within minutes, he'd gained the ocean and was paddling strongly through the waves. She'd watched until he was no more than a dot on the horizon. While her father shooed all the girls out from under the table and from their various hiding places in the house, Annie had sat down and eaten her cake. She'd also decided that she'd never, ever cut her hair. And she never had.

"And do you, Anna Sarah Delacorte, take this man to be your lawful husband?"

Annie blinked, suddenly realizing she'd missed most of the wedding service. Sam waited patiently at her side, not letting on by so much as a glance that her hesitation bothered him.

"I'm sorry," she murmured. "I was just remembering my sixth birthday party."

Sam gave her a tender smile. "Funny. I was thinking about that, too."

"You promised you'd marry me that day."

"And I always keep my promises, don't I, Annie?"

"Yes, you do." She turned to the preacher. "I do. I do take Sam."

"Have you rings?"

"'Fraid not," Sam admitted. "Wasn't quite expecting a wedding when I woke up this morning."

"Considering what you'd been doing the night before, you sure as heck should have!" Rolly called from the back of the church.

Myrtle stood. "Well, I have a ring you can have. It's about time it was used for its intended purpose." She leaned heavily on her cane as she joined Sam and Annie at the altar. "Consider it a wedding gift."

Annie opened her mouth to argue. But one look into Myrtle's eyes and the impulse died. "Thank you. I'll always treasure it."

Myrtle handed the ring to Sam. "Be good to her, or I'll have words with you."

"You know I will."

She smiled, running a loving hand along Sam's jaw. "Yes, I do. You always were a good boy."

With that, she stepped aside. Sam took Annie's hand in his and slipped the ring onto her finger. The preacher pronounced his final blessing and Sam gathered her into his arms. The kiss he gave her was a sweet promise, one she returned with all her heart. The instant he released her, they were surrounded by well-wishers. Apparently, now that they were properly wed, all was forgiven.

She expected to see a hint of annoyance from her new husband. But he surprised her. When Rolly teased him about being a shotgun bridegroom, Sam shook his head. "All you did was force Annie to fulfill her promise. If anything, she's a shotgun bride."

Pansy appeared then, drawing Annie off to one side. "Are you all right?" she asked. "Bertie insisted this was what you wanted—"

Annie lifted an eyebrow. "How would he know that?"

"He said it was obvious."

"Well, you can tell Bertie—"

"That he's absolutely right." Sam dropped a heavy arm around her shoulders. "Isn't that what you were going to say, Mrs. Beaumont?"

Mrs. Beaumont. She shivered. They'd attracted a small crowd, all of whom were waiting to see how she'd answered. She hesitated, aware that several of those in the group were less than sympathetic toward Sam and would be only too happy for his new bride to say something disparaging. "I've always wanted to marry Sam," she said simply.

The mayor frowned. "Then why didn't you? Why did you have us…" He broke off, his face growing more ruddy than usual. "You know."

"Because I was young and foolish." And her father had found an effective method of stopping her. One that continued to hang over her head like the Sword of Damocles.

"It was a misunderstanding," Sam interjected in a tone that no one could mistake. One that warned: Argue at your own risk. "It's been resolved, which is all that matters."

"The saint and the sinner," the mayor pronounced with a hearty laugh. "Should make for an interesting marriage, wouldn't you say?"

Bertie cut into the circle. "Sorry to break up the wedding, folks. But I just heard. The hurricane's changed direction. At last report, it's picked up speed and is headed right for us."

CHAPTER NINE

As soon as news of the hurricane spread, people offered their good wishes and began departing the church. Annie turned to Bertie in concern. "How much time do we have?"

"Not a lot. Better start boarding up now. We'll be in the thick of it by sundown."

"We weren't able to hear any updates last night," she said, struggling to stem the revealing color that blossomed across her cheekbones. "Where is it? Has it strengthened?"

"The winds are over a hundred, Annie. It's going to be a bad one. You can already see some of the outer bands of the storm to the south of us."

Myrtle joined them, leaning on her bird-of-paradise cane. "I'm going on home, dear. Those nice young boys you've been tutoring have volunteered to come over and close up my shutters and make certain the house is watertight."

"Where are you going to ride out the storm?" Annie asked in concern. "Maybe you should stay with us at Soundings."

Myrtle's dark eyes held a teasing glint. "Now that would make for an interesting wedding night."

"Looks to be an interesting wedding night regardless," Sam replied dryly. "You know you're welcome to come home with us."

"No need, my boy. Pansy and Bertie have made a similar offer, which I've accepted."

"But they're on the ocean," Annie fussed. "They always get it worse than we do."

Myrtle thumped her cane in exasperation. "Heavenly days, Annie Beaumont, you know that old Delacorte place has withstood every hurricane we've had these past thirty-some years. Now stop your worrying and let Sam get you home. I'm sure you two have enough to do without adding me to your list of concerns."

Annie Beaumont! It felt as odd as it did wonderful to hear her new name. It also felt appropriate, almost like coming home. In a rush of affection, she gently enclosed the older woman in a warm embrace. "I love you," she whispered. "You've been a mother to me all these years and I can't thank you enough."

"I love you, too, dear heart." Emotion trembled through the older woman. "You know I would have been proud to claim you as my own."

"Yes, I know." Wiping tears from her eyes, Annie released Myrtle and stepped into her husband's waiting arms. "Take me home, Sam."

"My pleasure."

He carefully adjusted the veil and circlet of flowers on top of her curls. Then before she knew what he intended, he swept her into his arms and carried her back down the aisle. Laughing, Annie peered over his shoulder and threw Myrtle a kiss goodbye. Outside, the first bands of rain could be seen marching toward them across a tainted sky. But directly overhead, it was blue and clear, with the sun still warm on their faces.

"Excuse me, Mr. Beaumont?"

Annie tensed, recognizing the voice. No! It wasn't fair. She should have been allowed a few days of marital bliss before it all came to a painful end. Apparently, she wasn't even to have that. "It's Pops's lawyer," she murmured reluctantly.

Sam set her down and turned to greet the man. "Come to congratulate me on my nuptials?" he asked.

"I apologize for the interruption." The lawyer looked truly sorry, too. "I've been instructed by my former client, Joseph Delacorte, to give this envelope to the fiancé of his daughter, Anna Sarah." He held out a thin white envelope.

"I'm not her fiancé," Sam replied mildly. "I'm her husband."

"Yes, sir. I appreciate that fact. I'm still to give you this." He offered the envelope again.

Sam frowned. "Just out of curiosity…how many of those things do you have stashed away in your office?"

"Pardon me?"

Sam gestured toward the envelope. "Letters from Joe. How many do you have? What if a building falls on me and Annie gets herself some brand-new fiancés? Do you have envelopes for all of them, too?"

"No, sir. I don't think Mr. Delacorte anticipated that possibility. There's just this one."

"I see." Sam lifted an eyebrow. "You know what the letter says, lawyer man?"

"No, sir. It was sealed when given to me." He held the envelope out for the third time. "Mr. Beaumont, I have a wife and kids at home. With this storm coming, they need me there to help prepare for the worst. As soon as you take this and sign for it, I can be on my way."

"Fair enough." Sam scooped up the envelope, folded it in half and stuck it in his pocket. Then he took the pen the lawyer offered and signed the slip of paper acknowledging receipt of Joe's letter.

All the while, Annie waited in silence, watching as any

chance of happiness disappeared into Sam's pocket. "Aren't you going to read it?" she asked the instant they were alone.

"Nope." He trained a weather eye on the approaching storm. "Our first priority is to get home and secure the house. We can worry about letters and secrets and dastardly deeds later."

She brightened fractionally. It looked like she'd get her reprieve after all. "I'm sorry you had to take so much teasing at our wedding," Annie said the minute they arrived at Soundings.

Sam shrugged. "It didn't bother me. I think you'll find I've become socially acceptable."

She turned and studied him in concern. "Why?"

"Because I married you, of course." She knew she paled. She also knew that Sam noticed. He paused by the front door and dropped heavy hands on her shoulders. "That tears it, Annie. What's the big secret? What's in that damned letter?"

"It explains that I'm not quite the saint most people believe."

"What did you do?"

She laughed, the sound edged with despair. "Nothing. That's the funny part. I haven't done a damned thing."

"You've tried, though. Why? So people won't think so badly of you when they discover your secret?"

"Yes."

"Was your sign wrong, Annie?" he asked gently. "Did you have an affair after I left. Is that it?"

"No," she hastened to assure him. "No sordid affairs. I wasn't interested in anyone after you." It was an honest, if telling, confession.

"Then what is it?"

"If you want to know, read the letter." She crossed

her arms in front of her and set her chin at a stubborn angle. "Otherwise, we have work to do and standing around yakking our fool heads off isn't going to get it done."

He slanted her a wry grin. "Something tells me we have two storms brewing. And I'm guessing the hurricane might be the easier of the two to handle."

"Is that your decision? We prepare for the hurricane?"

"That's my decision."

"Then let's get moving."

Without further ado, she shoved open the door. But before she could take a single step inside, he swung her into his arms again and stepped over the threshold. "This might not be the best time to break with tradition," he offered in explanation.

"Good idea." It amused her to realize his romantic gesture had left her breathless—especially when he didn't immediately put her down but cradled her close enough to feel the rock-steady beat of his heart. "I thought we had work to do," she felt honor bound to mention.

"We do." His lips caressed her temple before slowly drifting along the curve of her cheek. "But first things first."

"As soon as you put me down, I'll check the pantry to see if we'll need to lay in some supplies." She shivered, her head dipping back against his shoulder. "*After* we've taken care of first things first, that is."

"As soon as I put you down, you can also make sure we have plenty of water and batteries and canned goods." He nuzzled her ear, catching the lobe briefly between his teeth. "Candles, too."

It took a full minute to gather her scattered thoughts enough to reply, "I know what to do for a hurricane. I've lived here all my life, remember?"

"Humor me," he advised.

The edgy roughness in his voice startled her. Before she had a chance to question it, he covered her mouth with his. She wrapped her arms around his neck and clung to him, wishing with all her heart that their marriage was a real one. That Sam had proposed in the traditional fashion instead of having half a dozen shotguns do his proposing for him. And she wished that the letter her father had left wouldn't make a difference. Just when she was on the verge of saying to hell with everything and begging her Beaumont husband to take her to bed and make her his wife, he set her on her feet.

"Okay, Sam," she said, still bemused by his embrace. "I'll make a list of what we need. Then I'll head over to Drake's and pick up anything we're missing. What else do you want me to do?"

"I'll take down the screens and board up the windows if you'll gas the bikes. Secure *Lulubelle*, too. This storm's moving in fast, so I'm not sure how much time we'll have to get ready. Supplies come first, okay?"

"Got it."

Before she could do as he requested, he swept her into his arms again, holding her tight. "You should get off the island."

"It's too late, Sam. You know that. They'll be taking the ferries into harbor by now. Besides, I'm not willing to leave you."

He brushed her hair from her face. "Oh, yeah?" he said with a crooked smile. "And why not?"

"Because you're my husband."

"You still can't admit the truth, can you?" Did he even realize how he wound her hair around his finger? Or had it become so automatic a gesture that it escaped his notice?

"What truth?" As if she didn't know.

"You love me, Annie. But you're either too stubborn or too afraid to admit it." He framed her face and kissed her again, more deeply this time, with a desperate passion she couldn't mistake. "I was a fool to wait to make love to you. If we survive this storm, I'll correct that small oversight. And when I'm done, I'll rip down that damned sign and use it for kindling."

"You'd better," she whispered. "I really don't want to be the only married virgin in town."

"You won't be," he assured her, reluctantly putting her out of temptation's reach. "As much as I'd like to take you upstairs and slam the knobs off the bedroom door, we don't have time. Not for the sort of wedding night you deserve."

"It'll be all right, Sam. We've survived worse than this. We'll slam those knobs off soon enough."

"Don't tempt fate to prove you wrong, sweetheart." *Or me*, he might as well have added.

With a cheeky grin, she headed for the kitchen. She could feel his gaze on her back, watching her as though he had all the time in the world instead of a thousand chores piled up. She worked on sauntering. But it only made her hips ache and her hair bounce into an even more unruly tangle beneath the veil and garland of flowers she still wore. She also had the sneaking suspicion the choked sound he made was a bitten-off laugh. How deflating.

After packing away Pansy's veil and dropping the flowers into a bowl of water, Annie set to work. As the day progressed, she found she barely had a chance to catch her breath, let alone enjoy her newly married state. And with each fading hour, her list grew longer instead of shorter. Most worrisome of all, Annie noticed that Sam's mood was gradually disintegrating.

At first, she thought it was exhaustion. The plywood for boarding up the house was heavy and awkward and difficult to maneuver on top of a ladder. With so many windows to cover, it would tax a small army of workers. She even tried to attribute his edgy behavior to sexual frustration. His restraint last night on top of the unwelcome demands caused by the hurricane would try the patience of a saint. She should know, she thought with a scowl. It sure tried hers. Whatever the actual cause, it shredded Sam's self-control.

He never took his temper out on Annie, though. In fact, he said very little. But she couldn't help noticing how his mouth formed a taut line, as if he was fighting a constant battle to bite back careless words. And the look in his eyes worried her. The islanders had always described him as having wicked Beaumont eyes. She'd heard the joking reference practically from the day she'd been born. Heck, from the moment she'd first looked into them, she'd been utterly captivated. But today they contained a wildness that shocked her, reflecting the frantic expression of a caged animal desperate for a means to escape his prison.

Had marriage done that to him? she wondered uneasily.

Wisely, she chose not to confront him. Demanding an explanation would only release the beast from his cage and no doubt he'd rip into the first innocent to cross his path. The fact that she'd be that innocent didn't escape her notice. So she bided her time, continuing with the endless list of preparations still to be accomplished.

By late afternoon, the wind had picked up to the point it would soon be too dangerous to go outside. As a final chore, Sam rode the motorcycles into the boathouse. She could hear the powerful thunder of their engines as he gunned the throttle in order to get them up the steep ramp to the platform he'd hastily constructed to hold them. Unless the sound flooded above ten feet or the storm tore the roof off, they'd be safe enough.

"I think that's it," he announced as he entered the kitchen. He was filthy and exhausted, lines of strain etched deep into his face. If she hadn't known better, she'd have sworn he'd waded out into the sound and rolled around in the muck and mire.

"I'll have dinner ready the minute you're out of the shower."

"I'm not hungry." He eyed her damp hair. "I see you've already washed up."

She shrugged. "When the power goes, so will the water. I thought it might be a wise precaution."

"I'll get the generator as soon as we've recovered from the storm. At least that way we can run the water pump when the next hurricane hits us." He looked like he wanted to say more. Heck, he looked like he wanted to *do* more, which told her how high his adrenaline must be running. "Guess I'll head on upstairs."

He reappeared a short time later, dressed in clean jeans and a cotton T-shirt. His hair had been momentarily tamed, which provided a sharp foil to the static of primitive energy that continued to pour from him. They ate dinner, their silence at odds with the staccato pelt of heavy rain and the building howl of the wind. Every so often, they'd catch the sporadic clatter of heavy tree branches knocking against their neighbors. It would grow worse and they both knew it. Annie leaned forward and adjusted the flame on the hurricane lamp she'd lit in case the power went while they were eating. She'd used scented kerosene, hoping he'd find the subtle odor of lavender and lemon soothing.

"I filled the tub," he announced abruptly.

"Good. We'll need it for sponge baths. We have plenty of bottled drinking water. I've also put empty buckets in the foyer and a stack of old towels on the steps just in case we spring any leaks."

More silence. "I should check the doors and windows one more time," he declared suddenly.

"It'll keep until after you've eaten." Thinking he might argue, she selected a tender piece of chicken and hand-fed him. He ate as though ravenous. "Not hungry, huh?" she teased.

His eyes had that look again, the blackness so absolute it seemed to swallow the light. "You shouldn't be with me right now."

His comment caught her by surprise. "Why would you say such a thing?"

"It's not safe."

She stared at him, amusement vying with bewilderment. "Sam, you're my husband. Of course I'm safe with you."

Frustration radiated from him. "You don't understand, Annie."

"Then explain it so I will." When he remained stubbornly silent, she leaned forward, catching his hands in hers. "If you couldn't bring yourself to hurt me last night, what makes you think you might now?"

He carefully disengaged himself from her hold. "I'm not...myself. My control is shot. I'm not...I'm not thinking straight."

Her brows drew together. He'd been on edge all day, and as the storm approached, he'd grown progressively worse. Oh, good heavens! *The storm.* "You have storm euphoria, don't you?" she demanded.

His mouth tightened. "Myrtle told you?"

"Not that you have it, no. But I know that's her name for it. I'd never heard the term until Bertie started talking about how antsy Pansy gets whenever a hurricane comes through. Myrtle seemed familiar with the reaction."

"Antsy," he repeated. "That's a good way of describing it. It's like an itch I can't scratch."

"Oh, Sam," she murmured. "If it makes you feel any better, you're not the only one. She says it's quite common, but that it bothers some people more than others."

"It only happens with hurricanes," he said. "I think it's the extreme low pressure, though I don't know if they've done any scientific studies on the phenomenon. All I can tell you is that the more the barometer bottoms out, the more restless I get. For some it's euphoria. For others it's a sort of madness."

"And you're one of the others?"

"Yeah." He was silent for a moment, as though struggling to express what he felt. "The closer the hurricane, the worse it becomes. I can't think straight. Words become a jumble in my head. I can't settle. My emotions—"

"Get a bit edgy?" she suggested tentatively.

His laughter confirmed her guess. "A bit. I'm irrational. I make foolish decisions. Once, when I was fourteen, I tried to climb onto the roof to remove a tree branch at the height of the storm. Myrtle had to physically restrain me."

"Good heavens, Sam! You must hate it."

"It's the loss of control that I hate more than anything." He fixed her with a warning look. "So now you know. As the storm gets closer, I'll get worse."

She tried to temper his mood with humor. "It has the opposite effect on me. I get more and more sleepy."

"Sleep might be a good idea. You can curl up somewhere out of harm's way while I pace the floor."

"It gets that bad?" she asked sympathetically.

"Bad enough that compassion will only irritate the hell out of me."

A slow smile built across her face. "Was my compassion leaking? Sorry. I hate when that happens."

For an instant, amusement relaxed the lines bracketing his mouth. "And maybe you'd better not smile at me, either."

She lifted an eyebrow. "No? Why is that?"

"Because it'll tempt me to use you as a means to ease my tension." He shoved his plate to one side. "And that's no way for a bride to celebrate her wedding night."

"I thought that was the whole idea of a wedding night. To ease all those intriguing little tensions," she replied lightly.

"Not in my current mood, though I appreciate the offer." He kicked back his chair and stood. "If you'll excuse me, I'm going to check the house again."

Annie hastened from her seat and circled the table. She placed a tentative hand on his arm. "Is there anything I can do?"

The power flickered then, the lights briefly dimming before regaining their intensity. Sam gritted his teeth, the muscles across his jaw pulled taut. "No, thanks. Your best bet is to stay well clear of me until morning."

He backed away from her, his face falling into shadow. His hands were balled at his sides, the strain building within him as forcefully as the wind built toward full hurricane strength. She'd never felt so inept or uncertain.

He needed her. But she didn't know how to help him. She could go to bed as he'd requested. Or she could...

Silently, she slipped upstairs and waited until Sam's relentless pacing brought him into the bedroom with the infamous knobs. Trailing after him, she shut the door and turned the old-fashioned brass lock. The soft click brought him around.

"What are you doing?" he asked.

"I've decided to have myself a wedding night."

"I warned you that would be a bad idea." He held out his hand. To her dismay, she saw that it actually trembled. "Give me the key."

"I will. In a bit."

There was a loud pop as a tree twisted in two, then a thundering crash as it hit the ground. Instantly, the lights winked out. Annie pulled a small flashlight from her pocket and trained it toward the nightstand where she'd left candles and matches at the ready. A moment later, flames danced merrily, pushing the shadows to the far reaches of the room.

"Please, Annie," he whispered harshly, "you don't want to do this. Let me out of here."

"You need me, Sam. I can help."

"The smartest thing you can do right now is to lock that door with me on the other side of it. You gonna do the smart thing, wife?"

She held the key high enough for the candlelight to flicker off the brass. Then she dropped it down the front of her dress. "Does that answer your question?" Cautiously, she approached, keenly aware that he eyed her with a dangerous hunger. "You don't have to talk. Pace if it makes you feel better. I have a few things I need to take care of before we start."

Another tree crashed to the ground, this one farther

away. Even so, he flinched. "What things?" he asked as though desperate for a distraction.

She crossed to the rickety chair and prayed it had enough stick-to-it for one more usage. She lowered herself onto the edge, relieved when it held. "I did something today that I haven't done in ages," she announced.

He tried to stand still; she could see the effort he expended in the attempt. Gusts of wind beat against the house as though determined to hammer a way in. "What?" He prowled the length of the room. "What did you do?"

"I put on stockings."

He ran a hand through his hair, the heavy waves tumbling across his forehead, emphasizing his rakish appeal. "It's humid as hell, Annie. Stockings would be sort of foolish in this weather, I'd have thought."

"Maybe." She slipped off her sandals. "Course, these are pretty special stockings."

That held him in place. For the first time, he didn't seem to notice the shriek of the wind or the desperate clatter of the branches clawing against the side of the house. "Special how?"

"Special because they end at the thighs and require special equipment to stay up." She tilted her head to one side. "You know the special equipment I mean?"

"Garters. You're wearing garters?"

"Just like a fancy city girl." She held out a foot and flexed her ankle, contemplating her toes. "But maybe you're right. Maybe it is foolish to wear them considering this heat."

"Yeah." He swallowed. "Foolish."

Slowly, she inched up the hem of her skirt from calf to knee to thigh. Just far enough so the tops of her stockings and a bit of the white lace garter were visible. An

unholy crash sounded directly beneath the window. He
didn't even blink, which she took as a good sign. How
ironic that after all they'd been through, she'd end up
seducing him. "Shall I take them off?" She peeked at
him from beneath her lashes, making her voice as rich
and smooth as fine sipping whiskey. "Or would you like
to do it?"

"Don't." Two swift strides brought him to her side.
He fell to his knees. "I'll do it."

With a flick of his thumb, he separated garter from
stocking, his fingers grazing the softness of her thighs.
She gripped the arms of the chair so hard she fully expected it to fall apart in her hands. "Roll them down,"
she instructed. "Gently."

The silk caressed her legs like the wings of a butterfly.
Or perhaps it was his fingertips trailing from thigh to toe
that caused the sensation. "They're off," he said.

"I'm still hot. Aren't you?"

He lifted his head and looked at her, his incredible
black eyes filled with a desperate need, an unabashed
wanting that ran so deep it brought tears to her eyes.
"You're torturing me, Annie. I don't know how long I
can stand it before I take you. I don't want to hurt you,
but my control—"

"Shh." She pressed her fingers to his lips. "I'll take
care of you."

Catching his hands in hers, she drew them to the buttons that ran the full length of her dress, assisting him
each time his fingers fumbled. Before long, the final button slipped through the final hole. His breathing grew
strained, and as though unable to help himself, his hands
fisted in the two halves of her dress, preparing to tear it
from her. At the last instant, he faltered. She covered his
hands with her own and gently parted the dress, slipping

it from her shoulders to drape over the chair. She sat before him wearing nothing but two tiny scraps of lace and cotton.

"Your turn," she told him.

He struggled to pull off his shirt, and once again she was there for him, gliding the cotton across his flat belly when he'd have ripped it. She helped him push it up over an impressive chest and shoulders until he managed to yank it over his head. He was sheer delight to touch, the muscles firm and sculpted, the light pelt of hair covering his chest a delicious abrasion. His pants came next and she knelt in front of him, stripping him of the final trappings of civilization, awed by the powerful differences between man and woman.

Reluctantly, she stood and allowed him to remove the last of her clothes, as well. The brass key hit the floor with a melodic ping. Sam didn't bother to retrieve it and Annie smiled. Maybe he wasn't so desperate to escape as he'd thought. Somehow they found the bed, tumbling onto the cool cotton sheets. At one point, he found the small belly-ring scar and soothed it with his tongue. Storm madness became euphoria, growing stronger with each kiss and embrace.

From the moment he'd set foot on the island, he'd been bent on seduction. He'd teased and tempted, coaxed and promised. But in the end, it was she who seduced, teasing him with the warmth of her love. She who tempted him toward a dream fulfilled. She who coaxed him into forgetting everything but their feelings for each other. And she who promised an abiding love, keeping that promise with sweet kisses and tender caresses, gifting him with her heart and soul and, finally, with her body.

"I love you," she whispered into the wild winds that

swept through them. "I've always loved you and always will."

"My wife. My own."

As the hurricane bore down on them, he let the madness come. He called it, reined it, then rode the storm with the woman he adored more than life itself. That night, Annie wasn't ruined. Nor was she seduced or compromised.

That night, Annie was finally loved.

CHAPTER TEN

Morning came and with it the end to both the storm and Sam's madness. Annie watched as he eased from their bed and gathered up his clothes. Something crackled and he stuck his hand in his pocket and pulled out Pops's letter. It was crumpled and damp but had managed to survive both Sam's exertions getting the house ready for the storm and the hurricane itself. Considering he'd changed before last night's dinner, she found it telling that he still had the letter in his possession.

He quietly left the room and Annie scrambled from the bed, throwing on her clothes. She crept downstairs in time to see him head for the kitchen. Following, she hesitated in the doorway, a hand covering her mouth as she waited for Sam to open the letter. As she waited for her marriage to crumble.

Sam turned the envelope over in his hands a couple of times, his brow furrowed in thought. Then he crossed to the table and picked up a box of matches. Carrying both the letter and box to the sink, he removed a wooden match from the box and struck it against the cover. A flame leaped to life and he held it to the envelope.

"Wait," she whispered.

He turned, the match a fraction of an inch from the envelope. "I was going to burn it."

"I know." She slipped into the room. "Don't."

"You don't want to stop me, Annie." He dropped the burning match into the sink before it could singe his fingers and reached for another. "You're afraid this letter will destroy our marriage. There's nothing your father could say that's worth that. If there's something I need to know, you can tell me. Otherwise, it's not important.''

Her chin quivered. "He didn't mean to hurt me. He really didn't. It was the stroke. It…it changed him.''

"Let me burn it, Annie.''

She shook her head. "Those are his last words to me. I can't burn his letter without knowing what he wrote.''

"Even if it hurts you?''

"Yes.'' She crept to his side, allowing the strength of his arms to comfort her. Gently, she removed the matchstick from his grasp and set it aside. "Even if it hurts.''

His breath escaped in a drawn-out sigh. "Are you sure?''

"Positive.'' There wasn't room in her marriage for secrets. Either he loved her or he didn't. "Open it, Sam.''

He ripped the end off the envelope and extracted the single sheet of paper. He held it to the light and swiftly scanned what was written. Without hesitation, he handed it to her. "Read it, sweetheart.''

Her hands shook so badly it took two tries to grasp the typewritten note. "*Dear Sam*,'' it began. Tears filled her eyes, blurring the letters. "I can't believe it. He addressed it to you.''

"Somehow he knew.''

She blinked, but it didn't help. The tears wouldn't stop. "I can't read it. I…'' Her voice trembled. "I can't see it clearly enough.''

Sam eased the letter from her hands. "Then I'll read it to you. Come on, let's sit down.''

She started to take the chair next to him, but he pulled her onto his lap. Grateful for his unswerving tenderness, she rested her head against his shoulder. "What does it say?"

"It starts,

'Dear Sam, I'm assuming you're the one who will receive this letter.'

He must have known I wouldn't let you go easily." His eyes reflected a ruthless determination. "He was right."

No question of that. "Keep reading, Sam. I've waited so long. I don't think I can stand another minute."

"Easy, sweetheart. We'll get through this together. He says,

'First, I must apologize. I shouldn't have interfered in your relationship with Annie. I regret the pain I've caused the two of you. At the time, I thought my decision justified. In my opinion, she was too young, your age difference too great. I was dying and, selfishly, didn't want to lose her when you moved to New York. Unfortunately, I did anyway.'"

"I wish I could say he was wrong." She touched a corner of the letter. "But it did change our relationship. Maybe if I'd known how seriously ill he was, I'd have understood why he went to such extremes."

"Maybe." Sam didn't sound nearly as certain.

"Finish it. Let's get it over with."

"'She was going to leave with you, Sam. Her bags were packed and nothing I said would change her mind. And so I told her the truth about her mother, a truth I would have made public if she insisted on going after you. I regret that. She agreed not to elope but left home the next day and moved in with Aunt Myrtle. I hope someday the two of you will forgive me. And I hope your marriage is blessed with happiness.'

"It's signed Joe Delacorte."

"That's it?" She couldn't believe it. "That's all he said?"

"So now we're supposed to divorce, right?" Sam teased tenderly.

Tears clogged her throat. "But that's not all of it. He didn't tell you the rest."

He tossed the letter onto the table. "I can't seem to convince you, Annie. I don't need to know. Whatever secret your father revealed about your mother died with the two of them. It's in the past. All you have to worry about now is the future." He cupped her chin, lifting her face to his. "Our future."

"Do you mean that?" she demanded in a low voice.

"After last night, do you even have to ask?"

"Sam? Annie?" Bertie's voice came from outside, resonating with unmistakable urgency. "Come quick!"

They were on their feet in an instant, racing for the foyer. It took precious minutes for Sam to force open the front door, warped again from the storm. Bertie was leaning against one of the porch support pillars, clearly winded.

"What happened?" Annie demanded. "Is it Pansy?"

Bertie shook his head. "It's Myrtle. I ran here as quick as I could. So many trees are down, I had to leave my car about a mile back and hoof it."

"What's happened? What's wrong with Myrtle?"

"She went out on the porch during the storm to try and fasten a loose shutter. I didn't hear her slip out. When we finally realized she'd gone missing—"

"*What happened*?" Annie cut him off, frantic with

fear. Sam caught her close, but she fought free of his hold. "Where is she?"

"She's hurt, Annie. She got knocked on the head and is suffering from exposure."

"She can't die! She can't."

"Easy, sweetheart," Sam murmured. "No one said anything about dying. Panicking isn't going to help. I'm sure they're doing everything they can for her."

"You don't understand!" The breath sobbed from her lungs. "I have to get to her."

"Calm down, Annie." He grabbed her arm, refusing to turn her loose no matter how hard she fought. "Listen to me, dammit! Arriving in hysterics isn't going to help Myrtle. All it's going to accomplish is to upset her."

"They're doing the best they can," Bertie offered. "Pansy insisted I come get you, but to be honest there's not much you can do."

"There's one thing. I can go to her."

"Annie—" Sam began.

"You don't understand," she shouted, barely registering his words. All she knew was that the path between her and Myrtle was blocked and she'd do whatever it took to get past. "I have to get there!"

He still wouldn't release her. "Why, Annie? Why do you have to?"

"Because she's my *mother*!" She burst into tears, the words an aching whisper. "She's my mother, Sam. Don't you understand? I'm not a Delacorte. I never have been. That's my secret. That's what I didn't want you to know."

He closed his eyes, comprehension written in the exhausted lines of his face. "We'll take the motorcycles."

"The bikes. Oh, thank heaven." Annie flew down the steps. "Hurry, Sam. We have to hurry."

"Slow down, sweetheart. We'll ride together. Bertie can take the other Harley." He glanced over his shoulder. "Come on, Deputy. We stashed the motorcycles in the boathouse. I assume you can ride?"

In other circumstances, Bertie's bewildered expression would have been laughable. "Yeah, I can ride."

By the time Sam reached the boathouse, Annie was already there, tearing open the door. Part of the roof had been lost, but the motorcycles had escaped damage. She hovered impatiently to one side as Sam wheeled out the first bike, then went back for the second. Not bothering to wait, she climbed on and gunned the engine. Instantly, Sam ripped down the ramp and slewed the second Harley around in front of her, sand flying in his wake.

"You're not driving," he announced, his tone warning he wouldn't be opposed. "I'll get you to her, I promise. But you're riding with me, not on your own. Now hand the bike to Bertie and come on."

The minute she'd mounted behind him, he revved the engine, streaking off across the yard. It seemed to take forever. Every time they'd start to make progress, a downed tree would block the road and they'd have to find a path around it. A full hour later, they arrived at Annie's old home.

Emergency workers were gathered in the driveway, and with an exclamation of horror, Annie leaped from the bike and ran toward them. Sam let her go, allowing her the privacy she'd undoubtedly prefer. Bertie roared up beside him and cut his engine. For a long moment, neither of the two spoke. Finally, Sam eyed the deputy. "You're not to utter a word to anyone about what Annie said."

"I'm not a fool, Beaumont. I know when to keep my mouth shut."

"Glad to hear it." He waited a beat. "Because you've owed me for a long time and today I'm collecting."

Bertie's jaw clenched, a dead giveaway as far as Sam was concerned. "How do you figure?"

"Shall we start with that beating you gave me seven years ago?"

Hot color washed up Bertie's neck. "Yeah. Guess I do owe you for that," he said, not bothering with a denial. "When did you figure out it was me?"

"Had it confirmed about two seconds ago. Had it figured out the morning after you locked Annie and me in the boathouse."

Bertie didn't deny doing that, either. "How'd you know I was the one who attacked you?"

"When a few of the good ol' boys jumped me, you started pulling them off. In the process, you threw a punch or two and it looked...familiar."

Bertie's throat worked for a minute before he said, "I owe you an apology for that."

"Yeah, you do. You believed Pops's story, didn't you?"

"Stupid, huh? Thinking you'd switched your affections from Annie to Pansy."

"Real stupid." Sam's curiosity got the better of him. "Did Pansy know what you did?"

"Not then. I confessed to her when she was pregnant with Bert Junior."

Comprehension dawned and Sam released a short laugh. "I gather she didn't take it well."

Bertie sighed morosely. "Cried for six months solid. Said you'd come back and even the score one of these days. She was convinced you'd press charges and I'd end up in jail. Or you'd have me thrown off the police force.

I couldn't convince her you were more likely to beat the tar out of me and call it square.''

Sam didn't correct him on that score. Marrying Annie had one serious drawback. While it had gone a ways toward appeasing his hunger for revenge, it had also tied his hands. He didn't think his sweet wife would take it too well if he went around pummeling her in-laws. "I gather you were also the one who rigged the doorknobs that second time around?''

"Yeah. Guess I should apologize for that, too, as long as I'm at it. It just seemed too good an opportunity to miss." He shrugged awkwardly. "I sure didn't mean to trap the wrong woman in there with you.''

"You're just full of clever ideas, aren't you?''

"Aw, heck, Sam. It wasn't me. I read this really cute article in some Texas magazine a tourist left behind. Told all about how this kid bought a nine-dollar date for his mom and then tried to compromise the two of them so they'd have to get married." Bertie shook his head. "That kid was smart. Scary smart, you know the kind I mean?''

"I have a good idea.''

"Anyway, I thought since this kid was some sort of brain, I'd steal a page from his book. Compromising folks doesn't seem to set too well in Texas, but I figured it'd be a slam dunk on Delacorte Island. Especially since it was Annie. She's sort of special. If somebody tries to mess with the town saint, they're gonna pay a steep penalty. Not that marriage to her would be much of a penalty," he hastened to add.

"I get your drift.''

Bertie cleared his throat. "So how is it, do you suppose, that Myrtle ended up being Annie's momma?''

Sam focused his attention on the crowd spread out

across Bertie's driveway. He thought he caught a glimpse of Annie's dress, but then it disappeared before he could be certain. "Good question."

"You figure she and old Joe...?" He shrugged awkwardly.

"I can't see Myrtle having an affair with a married man, can you?"

"Nope. Course, I can't see Myrtle having an affair at all." He brightened. "Maybe she went to a fertility clinic and Annie's one of those test-tube babies."

"I wouldn't go there if I were you, Bertie."

"Sorry, Sam." He inclined his head toward the group of emergency personnel. "Looks like they're waving you over."

"Actually, I think they're waving you over, Bertie."

Leaping off the motorcycle, the deputy swore beneath his breath. "It's Pansy. Hell's bells, she must have gone into labor."

Sam waited another minute before following Bertie into the milling crowd. He'd given Myrtle and Annie about as much privacy as he could stand. Time to tie up some loose ends. He found mother and daughter sitting off to one side. Myrtle's head was bandaged and she had a blanket wrapped around her spare frame. But other than that, she looked in surprisingly good shape.

"Hello, old girl," he greeted her affectionately. "What have you done to yourself?"

Myrtle thumped her cane in annoyance. "It's just a bump. Barely a scratch. But from all the hoopla, you'd think I was at death's door."

"Bertie certainly thought so."

"Bertie's an idiot," Myrtle opined with a snort. "Though I'll confess, it was my own foolishness that caused the problem."

Sam inclined his head. "Most problems are caused by foolishness. Or in some cases I know, pigheadedness." He leveled a gaze on Annie, ignoring her attempts to shush him. "Tell her, sweetheart. Tell her what you told me."

"It's nothing important," she insisted pointedly. "Nothing we need to trouble Myrtle about."

He released his breath in a gusty sigh. "She thinks she's a Beaumont, not a Delacorte."

"*Sam!*"

The shock on Myrtle's face was unmistakable. "What did you say?"

"Sam, please," Annie begged. "Don't."

"And she knows you're her mother, Myrtle."

Myrtle glanced at Annie, then back to Sam. Her cane wobbled violently. "How? Joe would never have told—"

"Not only did he tell her," Sam contradicted in no uncertain terms, "he threatened to tell the rest of Delacorte Island if she eloped with me."

"I didn't know." Myrtle lifted shaking hands to her mouth, her apprehensive gaze returning to Annie. "He swore when he and Martha took you in that he'd never reveal the truth."

Annie gently wrapped an arm around Myrtle's shoulders. "Why didn't you tell me? Were you ashamed?"

"No! Dear heaven, child, I'd have given anything to claim you as mine, to have raised you."

Annie visibly swallowed. "Why didn't you?"

Tears glazed Myrtle's eyes. "Joe didn't explain what happened?"

Annie shook her head. "Only that I was a Beaumont and you were my mother and that he'd publically disgrace you if I married Sam."

"Instead, you moved in with me."

"You were my mother," Annie whispered. "I wanted to be with you."

"Despite being a dreaded Beaumont?"

Annie lifted her chin in a defiant gesture. "I'm a Beaumont by birth and by marriage."

"Yes, you are that," Myrtle confirmed. "But you're also a Delacorte."

Annie clenched her hands together. "Joe?"

"No, sweetheart. I'd never have had an affair with a married man. It was Joe's brother, William. It was a story not unlike yours and Sam's. A Beaumont falling in love with a Delacorte. The families wouldn't have stood for it, despite our both being of an age." A smile flitted across her mouth. "At thirty-five, I guess you could say we were of an age and then some. Still, we met in secret. The difference from your situation is…we did elope. The ring I gave you at your wedding was the one Will would have given me had we married. It's all I have left of him."

"I'll always treasure it," Annie whispered, sliding her thumb across the wedding band.

Sam wrapped an arm around Annie, understanding the emotions that must be rioting through his new bride. This couldn't be easy for her, or for Myrtle. He glanced at the older woman.

"That's when you had your car accident," Sam guessed, connecting the pieces.

Myrtle nodded. "It shattered my legs and killed William. I woke up in the hospital pregnant, unwed and without the man I loved." She closed her eyes, rocking back and forth from the pain of her memories. "They didn't expect me to live, and quite frankly, I didn't want to. Only one thing kept me going."

"Me?" Annie asked softly.

"Yes, you, dear heart." It took Myrtle a moment to compose herself. "Joe was in the Coast Guard at the time, stationed not far from the hospital. He and Martha came to visit me in order to find out why Will and I were together in the car. When they learned of my condition, they suggested a solution."

"Adoption?"

Myrtle nodded. "They'd been married for years without Martha conceiving. They said they'd claim the child as theirs. Since they weren't living on the island then, no one would be the wiser." Her mouth twisted. "They thought it was such a perfect solution. My reputation would be protected, Will's child legitimized and that wild Beaumont blood kept a deep, dark secret. No one would know."

"Why did you agree?" Sam asked.

"The doctors said I'd never walk again, that I'd be confined to a wheelchair. I was a schoolteacher, a position I'd undoubtedly have lost when my condition became apparent."

"They could fire you for being a single mother?" Annie asked in shock.

"Twenty-five years ago? I suspect they could. More likely they'd have drummed up an excuse for letting me go, but the end result would have been the same. With no means of support, how was I to raise a child?" She rested her chin on the back of the hand holding her cane. "To be honest, I could give you all the excuses in the world. But it boils down to one thing. I was afraid. Not of ruining my reputation. But of ruining yours, dear girl."

Annie tried a laugh, one that fell flat. "Everyone's been so worried about my reputation."

"Including Joe and Martha." Myrtle slipped her hand in Annie's. "Your father did a terrible wrong. But he loved you, Annie. I know he did. As far as I could tell, he never treated you differently from Pansy or Trish. If he was a little overzealous in trying to keep you away from Beaumonts, perhaps you can understand why and forgive him.''

''What about Pansy and Trish? Are they—''

''Adopted, too?'' Myrtle shook her head. ''A few months after taking you home, Martha discovered she was pregnant. Sometimes it happens like that.''

''So what now?'' Sam asked. ''Does this stay our secret or...''

Myrtle fixed her eyes on the horizon, setting her chin as though in anticipation of a blow. ''I'd be honored to claim Annie as my daughter. But I won't do anything to embarrass or shame her.''

''You could never do that,'' Annie assured her. ''The only reason I never said anything was because it wasn't my secret to reveal. I figured if you'd kept it quiet all those years, you had a good reason. I guess while you were busy protecting my reputation, I was trying to protect yours.''

Myrtle laughed through her tears. ''We're a couple of fools, aren't we?''

''Like mother, like daughter,'' Annie said, swiping at her own eyes.

''Is it settled, then?'' Sam asked.

''Somehow I doubt that.'' Myrtle gave Annie a little push. ''I think you two have some final matters to settle between you.''

Sam grinned. ''I think you're right.'' Catching Annie's hand in his, he drew her off to one side.

Bertie rushed past them. ''Stay calm, folks! There are emergency personnel on the scene with experience delivering babies. Stay calm!''

"Pansy? She's having her baby now?" Just as Annie was about to start after her brother-in-law, Sam stopped her the only way possible. He wrapped his arms around her and distracted her with a kiss.

"Well?" he asked several pleasurable minutes later. "Is everything out in the open now?"

"Just about." She peeked up at him. "I guess you're relieved that Myrtle isn't really your aunt—or any other close relative, aren't you?"

"More than you'll ever know."

She toyed with the top button of his shirt for a moment, speaking in a rush. "I owe you an apology or two."

"For what?"

"For not eloping with you seven years ago."

"Would you have if it hadn't been for Myrtle?"

She glanced at him, then quickly away. "I'd at least have given you the choice of whether you still wanted to marry me or not."

He pulled back slightly, frowning. "Do you think I'd have changed my mind?"

"Don't you get it? I'm illegitimate. Like…like your mother."

He swore beneath his breath. "And you thought I wouldn't marry you because of it?"

She compressed her lips to keep them from trembling. "You used to say that you'd never allow your children to go through what you did. That's why we never made love, because you didn't want your sons and daughters to suffer for the sins of their parents. But that's precisely what would have happened if we'd married." Tears started to her eyes. "What will happen."

"Are you worried about our children, Annie?" he demanded. "Are you concerned they'll suffer because of you?"

The tears spilled over. "Yes," she whispered.

"No, love. That won't happen. You and my mother are two different people. She was..." He sighed. "Let's just say she was the sweetest woman in the world, but she wasn't the town saint and never tried to be."

"Once people find out the truth about me, I might not be the town saint, either."

He smiled tenderly. "I think you'll find your sainthood intact."

"But you won't be respectable, not married to me."

"To hell with respectability. It's not nearly as fun as being disreputable. Besides, I'd rather have you."

"Are you sure? Really sure?"

He cupped her face, brushing away her tears with his thumbs. "Annie Beaumont, just for the record, I love you. I loved you when I thought you were Joe Delacorte's daughter, which is saying a hell of a lot. And I love you even more, if that's possible, knowing Myrtle Beaumont's your mother. You are the most generous, kindhearted woman I know. I fell in love with you when I was all of twelve and I expect I'll love you when I'm a hundred and twelve. I promise you. Our children will be proud to have you for their mother. And their friends will envy them their good fortune."

Her laughter was the sweetest sound he'd heard in a long time. "I love you, too, Sam." Her eyes glittered with mischief. "Despite your being a wicked Beaumont."

"I've got news for you. You're now a wicked Beaumont, as well." A sudden thought struck him. "Is that why you sold the Delacorte land your grandmother gave you?"

She nodded. "I didn't realize I was also a Delacorte since Pops neglected to tell me that part. I thought I was just a Beaumont. It didn't seem right somehow to own the property.''

''Sweetheart, with your coloring and appearance, how could you doubt you were anything but a Delacorte?''

''I don't know.'' She shot him a telling look. ''Maybe the Beaumont pride and stubbornness got in between me and the mirror.''

''Hmm.'' He tucked her close. ''I think we'll have to work on those particular character traits. You don't seem to quite have the hang of being outrageous.''

''Give it time. I'll learn.''

''I have every confidence in you. But promise me one thing.''

''What's that?''

''Absolutely no spikes.''

''Fair enough.'' She wrinkled her nose in thought. ''How do you feel about nipple rings?''

''Do you mean to tell me that after that belly scar, you'd even consider—''

''Not for me!'' She grinned. ''I was thinking for you.'' He drove that thought clean out of her head with a kiss that left her as breathless as it did hungry for more. ''Can we go home so I can show you how much I love you?'' she asked. ''Are we done here? No more secrets?''

No more secrets? He glanced toward Bertie and grinned. ''Well...no secrets worth mentioning!''

EPILOGUE

"WELL, boys? What do you think? We did a fair to middlin' job, wouldn't you say?"

"We saved Annie, which is the important thing," Ben concurred.

Rolly snorted. "Even if she did end up stuck with that Beaumont boy."

"Maybe that's not so bad," the mayor ventured. "After all, she is half Beaumont herself."

"Don't know why we didn't recognize that right off. She's a bit of a wild thing."

"Yes sirree," Rolly agreed. "Has those wicked Beaumont eyes, even if they are blue. You'd have thought we'd have seen that."

"And no wonder she's a saint. Look who her momma is."

The mayor chuckled. "Good blood will show."

Rolly ran a hand along his jawline. "You know…maybe Miss Annie will end up naming her babies after us."

"Have you lost your ever-blessed mind?" Mayor Pike demanded. "Why in tarnation would she do that?"

"Because she's so dang grateful for all we did matching her up with that Beaumont boy." The sheriff tugged the pistol from his holster and gave it a quick rub with his handkerchief. "Rolly Beaumont. Has a ring, don't you think?"

"I think we're going to have our hands full with those babies. Especially if they're as wild as the parents."

183

Ben's eyes widened in alarm. "I hadn't thought about that."

"Yes, sir," the mayor said. "They're going to need a very special sort of help."

Rolly surged to his feet. "All for one!" he shouted.

"And one for all!" the others chorused.

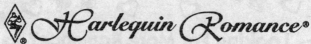

Harlequin Romance®

**brings you four very special weddings to
remember in our new series:**

WHITE
WEDDINGS

True love is worth waiting for....

Look out for the following titles by some of
your favorite authors:

August 1999—SHOTGUN BRIDEGROOM #3564
Day Leclaire

Everyone is determined to protect Annie's good name and ensure
that bad boy Sam's seduction attempts don't end in the
bedroom—but begin with a wedding!

September 1999—A WEDDING WORTH WAITING FOR #3569
Jessica Steele

Karrie was smitten by boss Farne Maitland. But she was
determined to be a virgin bride. There was only one solution:
marry and quickly!

October 1999—MARRYING MR. RIGHT #3573
Carolyn Greene

Greg was wrongly arrested on his wedding night for something he
didn't do! Now he's about to reclaim his virgin bride when he dis-
covers Christina's intention to marry someone else....

November 1999—AN INNOCENT BRIDE #3577
Betty Neels

Katrina didn't know it yet but Simon Glenville, the wonderful doctor
who'd cared for her sick aunt, was in love with her. When the time
was right, he was going to propose....

Available wherever Harlequin books are sold.

HARLEQUIN®
Makes any time special.™

Look us up on-line at: http://www.romance.net

HRWW

Celebrate **15** years with

HARLEQUIN®

Makes any time special ™

In celebration of Harlequin®'s golden anniversary

Enter to win a *dream!* You could win:

- A luxurious trip for two to
  The Renaissance Cottonwoods Resort
  in Scottsdale, Arizona, or

- A bouquet of flowers once a week for a year
  from **FTD**, or

- A $500 shopping spree, or

- A fabulous bath & body gift basket, including
  K-tel's *Candlelight and Romance* 5-CD set.

Look for **WIN A DREAM** flash on
specially marked Harlequin® titles by
Penny Jordan, Dallas Schulze,
Anne Stuart and Kristine Rolofson
in October 1999*.

FTD

**RENAISSANCE.
COTTONWOODS RESORT**
SCOTTSDALE, ARIZONA

K·TEL

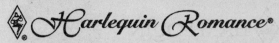

Harlequin Romance®

We're proud to announce the "birth" of a brand-new series full of babies, bachelors and happy-ever-afters: ***Daddy Boom.*** Meet gorgeous heroes who are about to discover that there's a first time for everything—even fatherhood!

We'll be bringing you one deliciously cute ***Daddy Boom*** title every other month in 1999. Books in this series are:

Who says bachelors and babies don't mix?

Available wherever Harlequin books are sold.

HARLEQUIN®
Makes any time special.™

Look us up on-line at: http://www.romance.net

HRDB1-R

Coming Next Month

#3567 TRIAL ENGAGEMENT Barbara McMahon
It was Mike Black's job to keep Candee safe until she testified in court—
and his idea of protection was hiding out with her at his brother's ranch
and pretending she was his fiancée! Candee was attracted to Mike, but
he knew better than to get involved with her, however hard she was to
resist...

#3568 ONE BRIDE DELIVERED Jeanne Allan
Cheyenne's response to a newspaper advertisement looking for a
mother led her to an orphaned boy and his uncle, Thomas Steele.
Thomas clearly had no place in his life for family or for love. But
Cheyenne knew that if she could draw out the softer side to his nature
he'd make the perfect father—and husband!

Hope Valley Brides: *Four weddings and a family!*

#3569 A WEDDING WORTH WAITING FOR Jessica Steele
Karrie had been the envy of all her colleagues when they found out she
was dating company executive Farne Maitland... But Farne was a man of
the world, while Karrie's upbringing had made her determined to be a
virgin bride. There was only one solution—marry and quickly!

White Weddings: *True love is worth waiting for...*

#3570 AND MOTHER MAKES THREE Liz Fielding
When James Fitzpatrick mistook Bronte for the mother who had
abandoned his little girl, Bronte realized he must have confused her
with her career-minded sister. But James was so handsome, and his
daughter so adorable that Bronte couldn't resist slipping into the role.
What would they do when they discovered that Bronte wasn't quite who
she seemed?